LIGHTS, CAMERA, CROSSCHECK

LIGHTS, CAMERA, CROSSCHECK

L. WOOD

*For my fellow hopeless romantics that don't necessarily
believe in love but still dream about this
kind of love finding them*

CHAPTER 1
ELIZA

I lean back from my computer and let my eyes focus on nothing. Sometimes when editing I completely forget to take a break and let my eyes rest, because I get in the zone. It also doesn't help that I'm running really close to my deadline before needing to send the locked cut off to the rest of the post team. My director also keeps wanting to change things last minute, mostly nit-picky things now. Which I don't have a problem with, because it's literally my job, but it does make things more stressful in the end.

All I have to do is get the okay from the director and I can export this film. Though I might seriously scream if he wants to change anything else.

Brian, the director, walks into my editing room, taking the seat next to me. This is my first time working with him. The other two directors that I usually work with typically just let me do my thing. They trust me enough that they really on sit in on my editing sessions when there's a scene that might need to be cut, or if we need to workshop the flow together. But with Brian, I've had to get used to another person being in the room with me during the whole editing process. I've also had to get used to the fact that he trusts me enough to put his film together, but not enough to let me be, which is totally fine especially with this being our first time working together.

"How are things going Liz?" he asks me.

"I fixed what we talked about yesterday, so now I just need you to okay it and I'll send the locked picture off to the rest of the team," I reply turning back to the monitors.

Brian lets out a sigh and says, "I'm sorry for making you fix the edit so many times, Eliza. I just want it to be perfect."

"Brian," I tell him truthfully. "It's okay. This is your passion project, your baby. And you entrusted me with it. It's my job to make sure it all comes together the way you want it to."

He takes a deep breath and nods.

This is a conversation that we've had many times before, but I don't mind reminding Brian that it's okay to let others do their jobs.

Brian is a relatively new director, so he's still getting used to the fact that he's working with people that actually want to do their jobs. It takes a long time to be able to be comfortable letting go of the reigns in this industry and delegating to other people.

I admire that he's been able to do this and fall into his directing role with relative ease. I know from my own experiences that not everyone is like that. Hell, the one time I directed a project both me and my first assistant director were having to take on roles that we shouldn't have had to do. While it was only a student production, it was still extremely nerve-wracking for me.

After showing Brian the newest version of his film, I turn to him and ask, "Picture lock?"

I hold my breath, because we've played this game multiple times already. I honestly won't be surprised if we don't lock the cut.

Surprisingly he turns to me, smiles, and replies, "Picture lock."

"For real?" I ask.

He nods, saying, "For real."

I clap my hands together and exclaim, "Hot damn!"

I turn to the monitor and say more reserved, "All right, I'll start getting *Last Night Avenue* ready to send to color and sound. And I'll send it off first thing in the morning."

"Awesome," Brian replies. "Do you have any plans for the rest of the evening?"

I glance at the clock to see that it is only 3 o'clock. If I time everything right I can catch the game for the Flames tonight, Atlanta's NHL team.

"Um yeah," I say, not thinking anything of it. "I'm hoping to catch a hockey game."

"You like hockey?" he asks, genuinely surprised. "I didn't think you liked stuff like that."

Not really paying attention to exactly what he is saying I reply, "Oh yeah. Grew up as a big football fan, but then discovered hockey a few years ago and have loved it since."

"That's interesting," he tells me. "I've never been to a hockey game before. Wasn't ever really a sports kid."

"I have an extra ticket if you'd like to go. My dad and I have been season ticket holders for a couple of years now, and we never end up using all of our buddy passes, even between the two of us."

"Seriously?"

I look at Brian and reply, "Yeah, of course."

"And you don't think that it'll be weird for the two of us to be hanging out after work?"

"I mean I don't see why it would be. I think we get along fine, and we're both adults."

"Okay, well I'm gonna go home and change really quick," Brian says before getting up.

"I'll text you the address for the arena and meet you there," I reply, turning back to the monitor to finish what I was doing.

I hadn't planned on inviting Brian to tonight's game, but it kind of just happened. My plan had been to go to the game by myself, enjoy an overpriced beer, and watch the hell out of my favorite team. I guess now I just have a plus one to keep me company, which I'm not totally upset about it. If anything inviting Brian to the game keeps me from being lonely, since I don't think my dad will be able to make it tonight.

CHAPTER 2
ELIZA

Stepping out of my Jeep with my black and lime green Flames jersey on feels almost like coming home, as strange as that sounds. I guess it's really just one of those things that I can't really explain. But man, I love everything about hockey; the chill of the ice, the sounds of sticks slapping pucks. Everything about the Kenshaw arena is super comforting.

My brother would say I'm a weirdo for thinking that, but Zeke also grew up on a football field, so he doesn't have much room to talk.

As I head to the door to wait for Brian, I take in the sights around me. So many people talking about tonight's game. It's the home opener, so there's a lot of excitement going around, because this means it's officially hockey season again.

"Wow this is a lot of people," Brian says coming up on my left.

As someone that isn't big on crowds, I sure do love a hockey crowd. There's just something about it that I can't fully explain.

I smile and ask, "Can you feel the electricity in the air?"

"I feel something," he says slightly skeptical.

I keep smiling and reply, "Come on."

I've been here enough times over the years that I don't have to stress about where I'm going.

After getting our tickets scanned and going through security we make our way to the food. Which is super nice, because it means that I can just enjoy things.

"Since you so graciously let me use one of your tickets, food is on me," Brian says as we step in line.

"Are you sure?" I ask.

"Yes, I'm sure."

"Well at least use my discount."

He nods and steps up to order. When it comes to my turn I order and glance at the candy.

"Anything else?" the cashier asks.

Quickly I grab a pack of Reese's and set them on the counter.

I've only been to one hockey game where I didn't have a coke and a pack of Reese's, and it felt so wrong. It's just a little tradition me and my dad have when we come to games, and I like to stick to it even when he's not here with me.

The funny thing is I always try to make my Reese's last for most of the first period, but my dad has usually scarfed his down before puck drop. It's something that we always end up laughing about.

As we get our food I lead the way to our seats. When my dad got the season tickets the first time, he wanted to sit at the top of the arena, so he didn't have to worry about pucks or players flying at him. I on the other hand wanted to be right there with the action and sit on the glass. We settled by choosing seats that were two rows back from the glass.

As Brian and I sit down he asks, "So is there significance to you wearing twenty-six on your jersey? Is it for a sibling or for your boyfriend perhaps?"

"Ha, no," I reply taking a bite of my burger. "No, I don't have a boyfriend, and my brother plays football."

"So, there's no significance?"

"Well, my brother always says that twenty-six is our lucky

number, but Ryan Ramirez had his first shutout of his career the night I saw my first hockey game."

"Remind me what a shutout is," Brian says in a questioning way.

I reply, "A shutout is when one team wins the game without the other scoring at all."

"I'm sorry if I ask a lot of questions during the game," Brian says.

I wave him off and reply, "No worries. It's like I tell my dad when I'm talking about film stuff with him: don't be afraid to ask about something if you don't know what I'm talking about."

He nods with no further questions at the moment.

By the middle of the second period, I am fully into the game.

One of the refs calls a bad call on one of our players, and I boo the referee along with the rest of the arena.

As our player skates toward the penalty box I yell, "Oh come you fucking idiot! If you aren't gonna call that on the Devils, then you can't call it on us! High sticking my ass, his stick barely left the ice."

"Definitely never thought you could get this worked up," Brian says.

I plop back down into my seat and reply, "Sorry. Bad calls get me worked up."

He lets out a small laugh and says, "I can tell."

The game continues on after my outburst, the refs oblivious to the fact that I just yelled at them.

I sit back and ask Brian, "So how are you enjoying the game?"

"I see why you like this. It's exhilarating," he answers.

I nod and turn my attention back to the ice just as one of the Flame's players is smashed into the glass in front of us.

Without meaning to I lock eyes with one of the most beautiful guys I've ever seen. His piercing blue eyes lock onto mine, his skin sun kissed as if he spent a lot of his summer outside, and black hair curling up around the bottom of his helmet.

This man has me completely frozen in place as we stare at each other. It's as if nothing else exists; not time, not other people, anything, and I can't say I've ever experienced anything like this before. The spell is broken when one of his teammates bumps him in the shoulder, forcing him to look away.

I don't know who he is, and I definitely don't recognize his name when he turns around. He had to have been traded to the Flames this season. I'm frozen in place as my eyes move down and register that he is now sporting the number 26.

I quickly look around, because that can't be right, Ramirez is number 26. I don't see the name Ramirez anywhere on the ice. Which doesn't make a whole lot of sense because I'm ninety percent sure that I didn't miss any trade announcements, but then again, I have been pretty busy the past few months. So, what the hell is going on?

Which okay, I realize that if Ramirez isn't in goal I likely wouldn't see him on the ice, but that doesn't really answer my question.

CHAPTER 3
REMINGTON

At the start of the preseason, I never expected for the Arizona Sabers to trade me. After all I've spent the last four years of my NHL career playing for them and helping to get them to the playoffs consistently.

When coach pulled me aside to tell me that I was going to be traded I was fucking angry, to say the least. I almost punched a hole in the wall but decided to use my anger on the ice.

Once I got over the initial shock and anger, all I could do was pack my shit up and move across the country. At least it brought me back to being closer to my family.

I've now been playing with these guys for a total of three months, and I'm still struggling to remember everyone's names but I'm trying.

"Yo, Ratatouille!" Jake Smith, one of my newest teammates and one of my only friends, so far, on the team yells. "First game in the ATL! You excited?"

"Nothing I haven't done before," I reply as I tighten up my skates.

To be honest I'm one fucking fart away from shitting myself, which would not be welcome at all.

Even though I've played in preseason games and been in

practices with these guys, I'm still nervous about how we're all going to play together in an actual game.

Closing my eyes I mentally chant to myself; *Speed I am speed. One winner, forty-two losers. I eat losers for breakfast.*

Now I know what you're thinking, and you're right, I am a grown man chanting a line from a kids movie. My nephew is at the age where I can finally show him one of the greatest animated films of all time, *Cars*. And to say that we've seen it a shit ton of times is an understatement.

You see when Max, my nephew was born, I had been watching *Cars* when my baby sister, Georgia, called me. So since then, it's been worked into my pregame routine, because for some reason it seems to get me in the right mindset to play sixty minutes of hockey. While also being a sort of tribute to my nephew, even if he doesn't know.

Standing up I shake out my muscles and jump exactly three times. Say what you want but hockey players are fucking superstitious and don't let them tell you otherwise. Some might try saying that they aren't, but at the end of the day we're all more stitious than we'd like to admit.

As we line up in the tunnel I can feel the electricity in the air, and my blood is pumping. Nothing like playing for the home crowd.

"All right?" Grant Sanders, our captain pats me on the shoulder.

I nod and reply, "I fucking love home games."

He smiles and moves down the line asking each of my teammates the same thing.

I'm ready to hit the ice and show Atlanta what I'm made of. And I hope like hell they are ready to see what *I'm* made of.

By the end of the first, we are down two points, and all of us are beating ourselves up over something. I know that each one of my teammates thinks that they could've done something differently, because that's my thought process. It doesn't help that the refs keep calling shit calls on us. At one point when I was heading into the sin bin, I could barely make out a woman calling the refs out on their bullshit, not like the woman could be heard. I'm honestly surprised that I was able to hear her as well as I did.

So, when we head back out for the second period, we are determined as hell to even the score and hopefully bring it home in the third.

As the ref blows his whistle and sets down the puck, I watch as my team wins the face off and starts down the ice. Moor, one of our forwards, sets up to take the shot but one of Dallas's players is able to steal the puck from him.

I hop up from the bench ready to get on the ice with the rest of my line. The second my skates touch the ice I go after the Dallas player, checking him as I get to him. In retaliation another of Dallas's player's comes up behind me and slams me into the glass.

Taking a second to get my bearings my eyes wander into the stands, and I happen to lock eyes with one of the most beautiful women I have ever seen.

Her curly hair is tousled as if she keeps running her fingers through it, and it has an almost reddish tint to it. I am curious about the actual name of the color of her hair, which is not something I normally care about. From my vantage point on the ice, I think I can faintly see a smattering of freckles across the bridge of her nose. And her eyes, don't get me fucking started on those eyes. I can't tell exactly what color they are from here, but I know if I saw them up close, I'd be able to tell and get so lost in them.

As my eyes rake over her I can tell that she is tall, which puts my head into overdrive. Tall women are something else.

I bet her legs go on for days.

"Yo Milly, you good?" Misha, one of my teammates asks as he bumps my shoulder.

I reluctantly break eye contact with the woman, and nod trying to get my head back in the game.

The entirety of the rest of the game I can't get her out of my head. Which is bad because I need to focus on hockey, and not women right now while playing. I can't be thinking of ways of how to at least get her name, I have a game to play.

Something about her drew me to her, and I can't for the life of me figure it out. What scares me is that I desperately want to figure out why this stranger has such a pull on me. It is the last thing I need, but I know I won't be able to stop until I am satisfied.

CHAPTER 4
ELIZA

"'ll be back in a few minutes," I tell Brian as I start to stand. "I need to go to the restroom."

"Just don't abandon me," he replies with a laugh.

I smile at him and shake my head as I head up the stairs.

I don't typically get up during a period, but I don't want to check about trades with Brian sitting there. I'm just glad the play was stopped when I decided to get up.

Stepping into a stall and locking it, I pull my phone out of my pocket and start my internet sleuthing. I'm not going to call it stalking because I'm utilizing public knowledge.

I pull up the Flame's Instagram and start scrolling until I find what I'm looking for. Those blue eyes—that I'm now realizing have more green than blue to them—staring at me through my phone screen. He is even more beautiful up close, but this picture doesn't really do him any justice. I can already tell just from the brief glance I got.

Moving my eyes away from his face I start to actually read the graphic, which reads:

Remington Miller #26 traded to the Atlanta Flames from the Arizona Sabers.

Well, that answers one of my questions, but not the one I am most curious about.

Swiping out of Instagram I pull up the Flame's roster, because I know that will tell me if Ramirez is still on the team or not.

Scrolling down to the goalie section I read the first name, then the second, and finally the third.

"Well shit," I say out loud without really realizing it.

"That's often what happens in the bathroom," the lady in the stall next to me replies.

I let out a sharp laugh before apologizing.

I swipe back over to Instagram and scroll until I see Ramirez's face. Dreading what I already knew I click on the graphic. He'd been traded to the Calgary Predators.

Dammit, I really hate trades, especially when I'm unaware about them.

Sighing, I close the app and replace my phone in my pocket. After exiting the stall, I wash my hands even though I didn't actually use the bathroom, and head back to my seat for the rest of the second period.

"Didn't you say Ramirez was number twenty-six?" Brian asks me as Miller skates by possibly on purpose but unlikely.

"Yeah, but he was traded to the Predators." I reply as nonchalantly as possible. "So now we have Miller sporting twenty-six."

"You didn't know that before going to the bathroom?" he asks joking. "Did you?"

I laugh and reply, "No. I've been so invested in editing your film that I haven't been scrolling on Instagram as much. So, I guess I missed the announcements. Was I that obvious?"

"I mean not really, but I have been working closely with you for the past four months, so I've kinda learned how to read you."

I take a sip of my beer and let out a short laugh.

"You wouldn't think that I'd care that much," I tell him. "But Ramirez was my favorite on the team, even if he was the goalie."

"You don't have to explain, I completely understand. We all get attached and care about things."

"I kind of think of it like how my favorite Robin is Jason Todd and how DC treats him," I reply nodding. "They don't know what to do with him, and always end up making him the angry Robin that's hell bent on making Bruce pay, even though it has been established that he has moved past that."

"Oh yes! Or how they want to make Bruce out to be this terrible father, when he isn't."

"Yes! You get it!"

As the third period starts, I can relax more. I didn't realize there was some awkward tension between me and Brian until he made the bathroom comment, but once that tension was released, we've been a lot easier going with each other.

That night when I get home, I'm looking at the trade announcements again, only this time I decide to see if they tagged Miller. Luckily for me they did—makes things easier to stalk his page—and go to his account.

I look at a couple of his posts before hovering my thumb over the follow button.

What do I have to lose? It's not likely that'd he'll see he has a new follower. I've done this many times before.

Just when I have about talked myself out of it, I think *what the hell*, and press the follow button.

CHAPTER 5
REMINGTON

I watch as she says something to the guy next to her and gets up. I watch as she walks up the stairs with a huge lime green 26 on her back, only it isn't my last name. I don't know why that irks me, but it does.

For a good few minutes, I didn't think she'd return, but she eventually does.

When I finally get to skate by her again, I make sure that she has a good view of me. Out of the corner of my eyes I see that she is laughing at something the guy she is with is saying.

That should be me, I think.

The guy doesn't really look like a sports fan, but she definitely is. I briefly wonder if he's here to impress her. She isn't dressed like a puck bunny, and she watches the actual game more than the players. I want to learn everything about this girl, and I have no fucking idea why.

I mentally slap myself and make myself focus on the third period rather than a pretty woman in a fucking Flames jersey that just happened to catch my attention.

When the final buzzer sounds, we've won by two points.

I'm not sure what end of game celebrations look like with the team, so I just follow my teammates leads.

I quickly look back where I know she was sitting and am disappointed to not find her there anymore. I know I shouldn't be, but I am. It's irrational thinking on my part.

When we finally get back to the locker room, I start stripping out of my gear as quickly as I can. I hate being in it longer than I need to be. As I step into the shower my mind keeps wandering back to that woman. I know if I don't stop, I'm going to have a hard on, that I won't be able to take care of until I get home. Not only do I refuse to jerk off surrounded to my teammates, but I also refused to fuck my hand to a stranger that I saw in the arena. I need to know her name before that.

I just need to get home and try not to think about her. Easier said than done.

I step out of the shower with a towel around my waist and pick up another to dry my hair before slinging it into the laundry hamper. I get back to my stall and start putting on my street clothes.

"Ratatouille!" Jake Smith yells as he comes up next to me. "Got any plans for tonight?"

Yeah, I'm gonna go home and fuck my hand while thinking of the pretty woman I saw in the stands, I think.

Dammit that didn't take long.

"I'm gonna go home," I reply.

"First win at home, that deserves some celebration!" he exclaims.

"I also need to go feed my cat before he decides to take over the world, and then I'm going to sleep."

"Boring, but if you change your mind, we'll be at Chancey's," Smith says.

That's one thing I like about him; he never forces me to go out with the team. He understands that sometimes I just need to be alone and recharge.

I barely have the door to my apartment open before my cat, Krypto, is beating it down because he didn't get his food at exactly 7 o'clock.

"I know buddy. I'm sorry," I say to him as I kick off my shoes and start towards the kitchen.

Krypto starts rubbing up against me, and walking between my legs, giving me shit for not feeding him. I try to not trip on him and fall flat on my face.

I scoop him up and he immediately starts purring. I nuzzle my face in his stomach fur, and he happily kneads my head.

"I missed you too bud," I say putting him back down and scooping some food for him.

I walk back to my bedroom and flop down on my bed without turning on the lights. Pulling out my phone I start to scroll through Instagram to see if Georgia has posted anything new about Max. I know she'll send pictures of him to me, but I still like seeing them on Instagram.

To my surprise a new follower notification pops up, curious I click it. When it finally loads the profile, I am floored to see that it is the woman from the game.

For a couple of minutes, I just stare in shock, but when it finally wears off I start to actually look.

Her name is Eliza Fox. I glance over the blue film editor title in her bio and read what's under it. I laugh at the "just MacGyver it" that she has in her bio, because it is kind of quirky and kind of tells me what she's like.

I'm surprised to see that Eliza only has two story highlights. I click on the first one that is titled "me," thinking that it'd be a blurb about herself, but it is instead a bunch of memes. I laugh at every one of them. I guess she meant the "me" more as it is what her personality is like. But either way just from that I can tell she is funny as hell.

Next, I click on the bubble labeled "film," not thinking anything of it. I'm greeted with a bunch of movie posters, including one of my favorite movies made recently, *Down Comes*

Night. There are also a few shots of something on a computer. There is one picture with the writing "one year ago," but looking at the date it is actually from six years ago, and it has a YouTube link attached.

Letting my curiosity get the better of me, I click the link and am taken to a video titled *One Card.* It is only about four and a half minutes, but I watch the entire thing. It is both stupid and funny at the same time. When the credits roll, I realize that Eliza is listed as the writer, director, and editor.

Even more curious I go back to Instagram and follow the tagged post back to the original.

Looking through the pictures I see a younger version of Eliza. From what I'm able to gather this is her directing debut.

For another few minutes I look at what she has posted. In quite a few of her pictures she's with a guy, not the one she was with tonight, but he does look a little familiar. I make a mental note to see if she has the guy tagged, so I can try and gauge if she's single or not.

Without hesitation I follow her back and pull up a DM with her.

ME

Funny running into you on here.

I wait a few minutes before placing my phone on my night-stand. I'm not expecting her to respond or anything.

My phone lights up with a notification, surprising me.

ELIZA

Well I had your name, but you didn't have mine, and I feel like we had a moment. Unless I imagined that.

I smile and start to type before she sends another message.

ELIZA

Also I didn't think you'd see my follow
notification.

ME

Right place, right time

ELIZA

. We haven't even been properly introduced

ME

Remington Miller. But you can call me Remy.

ELIZA

Eliza Fox

ME

Nice to meet you, now I'm going to go to sleep
before my phone falls on my face.

I don't want to stop talking with her—we've only exchanged
a handful of words—but I am seriously close to my phone falling
on my face and that will hurt like hell.

Krypto hops up on my bed and curls up next to me. I'm
about to put my phone down when a new notification comes
through.

ELIZA

Good night, Remy. Don't let the bed bugs bite.

Smiling I put my phone down again and curl up next to my
cat. Within minutes I'm dead asleep.

CHAPTER 6
ELIZA

I don't know why I sent that, it's like something took over and just did it.

Before I can freak out too much my brother's name pops up on my screen as he tries calling me.

"Dickwad," I say as I am put through.

"Pee breath," he replies. "Quick question. Are you home?"

"Yeah," I respond. "Why?"

He doesn't answer my question instead he says, "Cool, thanks."

It takes me a second to realize that he just hung up.

Not even a minute later I hear the lock turning on my front door.

"Bastard," I say turning over on my bed.

Only my brother would come over this late. Even though it's not really late for me, but for him it is especially with it being the middle of football season.

A minute later he saunters into my room and plops down on my bed next to me.

"What if I had been naked?" I ask as my way of a greeting.

He resituates himself and replies, "Nothing I haven't seen before."

I roll my eyes and ask, "What if I'd had a guy balls deep inside of me?"

"Ew! I don't need the image of my baby sister having sex."

"I'm ten minutes younger."

"Still." I roll my eyes again and ask, "What do you want Zeke?"

"What I can't just come visit my baby sister whenever I want?" he asks, faking shock.

I give him a dead stare and reply, "Z, it's midnight. Don't you have a game tomorrow?"

"Yes, I do actually. That's what I wanted to talk to you about."

I motion for him to continue.

"Are you going to be there?" he asks.

"You know I go to all of your games that I can. So yes, I'll be there. We picture locked today."

Zeke lets out a whoop and exclaims, "Fucking finally! Didn't think you were ever going to picture lock on this one."

"Ha ha, very funny," I dead pan. "Tell me about it."

"Also is it cool if I crash here?"

"Wally going at it again?" I ask referring to his room-mate/teammate.

Zeke nods and replies, "Fifth time in the past two hours."

"Damn. Either they have stupid crazy stamina, or something is fucking wrong."

"My thoughts exactly."

"Yeah, you can crash here. You know where everything is."

"Want to watch a movie?" he asks giving me soft puppy dog eyes.

"No," I reply trying to ignore him.

"Why not?" he asks intensifying his puppy dog eyes.

"Because you'll end up falling asleep, and I don't want your smelly ass in my bed."

"Please. I'll get on my hands and knees to beg."

My 6'4, 210lbs NFL playing brother ladies and gentlemen.

"Fine," I reply as I roll my eyes. "Just don't steal my covers or I'll punch you."

"Thanks sis, you're the best!"

Not even thirty minutes into the movie and the fucker falls asleep.

Not wanting to sleep in the same bed as my grown ass brother, I throw the covers off myself and head to my couch. I have a guest room, but that mattress is way too soft for me.

Neither of us has ever been able to go to sleep super early, we're more night owls than anything. But ever since Zeke was drafted into the NFL his body hasn't allowed him to stay up as late as he used to.

Grabbing a blanket, I lay down on the couch and throw it over myself.

I decide to put a long play video on YouTube, and it isn't long before my eyes are getting heavy, and it is an effort to keep them open.

CHAPTER 7
ELIZA

"Someone named Remington is DMing you," my brother says as he sits on me.

Slightly startled, I blink a few times and rub my eyes as I try and process what is happening.

"Get off of me you fat ass," I say, sleep still heavy on my voice as I try to push him off.

"Someone named Remington is DMing you," he repeats.

I grab my phone out of his hand and click the notification.

I'm so glad that my face ID works, and that my idiot brother doesn't know my password. Though I guess it doesn't matter all that much, because I know he'll just be trying to read over my shoulder. The nosy fucker.

I blink the sleep out of my eyes and read the message.

REMINGTON

The bed bugs didn't bite. Thanks for warding them off.

I snort and Zeke asks, "Who is this and why are you telling them no to let the bed bugs bite?"

I roll my eyes and reply, "Mr. Overprotective."

"Eliza," he responds seriously.

"His name is Remington Miller," I reply as I start to type. "He plays for the Flames."

ME

Glad to hear.

Zeke whips his head to me and asks, "Why the hell are you talking to a hockey player? Better yet how did you meet?"

I love my brother, I do, but holy shit sometimes I want to actually strangle him. He acts as if I've never been with a guy in my life. Though he probably wishes I was a nun or something.

"I followed him not expecting him to reciprocate the follow. And I technically haven't met him, just locked eyes from the ice," I quickly rush out.

Zeke stares at me for a few minutes before exclaiming, "What the actual fuck Liz!"

I toss my phone at him and say, "Here if you're going to be like that read the messages."

I work in the film industry, and my brother is more dramatic than me.

"There's like five messages here," he says handing me back my phone.

"I know. It's just an interaction we had last night, drama queen."

"Were you ever going to tell me?" he feigns concern and shock.

"There is literally nothing to tell," I reply. "Now can I either make you breakfast or buy you some so we can forget about this?"

He taps his chin a few times as if in thought before saying, "Waffle House."

I sigh. "Okay, but I'm not getting yelled at by your nutritionist, again."

Yes, that has happened before. Zeke quickly fired that guy and hired a new one.

Zeke dramatically throws his arms around me and says, "You're the best sister ever."

"I'm your only sister, dipshit. Now let me go so I can get ready."

This is a tradition we used to have, the two of us at a Waffle House before one of his games. We still try to keep it up as much as possible, but it's difficult now that we're all grown up and not always in the same state.

By the time it's time to head the stadium for Zeke's game, I am a little excited. I've always loved seeing my brother play, it's just been a few games since I've been able to go because of my schedule.

Slipping on my jeans, I grab my brother's Atlanta Ravens jersey and throw it on. Looking at my shoes I can't decide if I want to go with my tried-and-true Chucks or my Vans.

I decide to switch it up and wear the Vans before heading out.

Once I get into the stadium I head towards our box. It's not really ours because we share it with a few other families, but you get the point.

I don't like sitting in the box because it feels like I'm taken away from the action and crowd, but my dad and I suck it up for Zeke. He's the same way our dad and I are so he understands, but these seats are guaranteed for us, so we don't complain too much.

When I walk in I can see my dad sitting where we usually sit, and walk over to him.

"I have a bone to pick with you," I say to him as I sit down and prop my feet up on the seat in front of me.

"Oh lord," my dad replies. "What'd he do this time?"

I don't even bother asking how he knew I'm talking about Zeke.

"He has no boundaries. He broke into *my* house, crashed in *my* bed, and made me pay for *his* breakfast."

My dad lets out a laugh and replies, "Liz you know Z has never known boundaries when it comes to you."

"You're telling me," I fake huff. "First, I had to share a womb with the guy, then I have to share a birthday with him. It's like he thinks that he just has free access to my life."

My dad laughs again. "And you call him the drama queen."

I fake huff again and switch gears. "I'm surprised I didn't see you last night."

"You went? I didn't think that you'd be able to."

"Yeah, I know, but luckily we picture locked yesterday and that meant I could have the evening."

"You should've told me, and I would've tried to get out of my meeting."

I wave him off. "It's okay. I ended up inviting my director."

He raises an eyebrow, but doesn't ask about it instead he goes with, "Did you have fun?"

I turn to look at my dad and reply, "Did Neil Armstrong walk on the moon? Dad, did you seriously just ask me if I had fun at a *hockey game*? I mean hell yeah I did, it's fucking *hockey*."

"Good. We'll have to catch a few games together."

I nod.

Turning to look back at the field I notice someone to my left, someone that I've never seen in the box. Someone who happens to be looking at me.

When I fully turn my head I once again lock eyes with Remington Miller.

CHAPTER 8
REMINGTON

When I woke up this morning, I hadn't expected to find myself at the Mercedes Bens Stadium for an Atlanta Ravens game. But Jake had texted me asking if I would like to go to this game with him and a few other of our teammates. Before really thinking about it I had said yes.

There are already a few people in the box when we get there, which isn't all that surprising. Walking closer to the field I notice a woman with reddish curly hair—who makes me think of Eliza —talking to an older man. Both are wearing #26 Fox jerseys.

I know that name is familiar, but I can't place it.

I don't really mean to, but I overhear some of the conversation. The woman is talking about—someone I assume is the man's son—breaking into her house and crashing in her bed. My first thought is she is one of the player's girlfriends or wives, but then she makes a comment about having to share a womb with the guy and figure sister.

I can't help the silent laugh racking through my body.

When the woman says something about hockey I turn to get a better look at her. Since she is turned away, I can't really see her face too well, but I have a feeling that I've seen her before.

When she turns to look in my direction I feel like I'm having déjà vu.

Holy shit! No wonder the last name Fox felt familiar to me, I'm staring at Eliza Fox. The woman that had caught my attention last night. The one that had found me on Instagram, and I had DMed on a fucking whim.

I smile at her as she says, "Holy shit!"

"What is it, Liz?" her dad asks.

She waves him off and gets up. I think she's going to walk out of the box, but instead she moves to sit next to me.

"Are you following me or something?" she asks jokingly.

"I could ask you the same thing," I reply through a laugh.

She claps back, "Considering this is my brother's football game, I'd say otherwise."

"Well, I didn't even know you had a brother or that he played football when I agreed to come," I reply through another laugh.

Since she's mentioned having a brother, I think about the guy in a good many of her posts and how he did bear resemblance to Eliza, so I think it's safe to assume that he's her brother.

"Liza?" her dad asks.

She replies, "Yes?"

The more she talks the more I can pick up on a slight southern accent, which is honestly hot as fuck. I've always been a sucker for a woman with a nice accent.

"Who's your friend?" he asks, amusement clear in his voice.

"Oh my god, you're worse than your son," she replies. "Remington, my father, Jeremiah. Dad, Remington. Happy?"

Reaching around Eliza I put out my hand for him to shake and say, "Nice to meet you sir. Though, I wouldn't really say I'm friends with your daughter since I technically just met her."

Jeremiah shakes my hand and glances between me and his daughter but doesn't say anything. I can see a knowing look in his eyes, though I think he is getting the wrong idea.

Eliza rolls her eyes and tells Jeremiah, "Please don't get any ideas, dad."

"I'm not," he replies throwing his hands up in defense.

I can't help the smile that is trying to take over my face.

She gestures to me and says, "He plays hockey. We've had one conversation before this."

I notice that she doesn't mention that it was one conversation through Instagram, but that is probably for the better. I don't know if anything will happen between us or if it was a fleeting moment. The only thing to do is see where things take us.

Jeremiah's eyes twinkle before he teases, "Oh so this is the boy Z said you've been texting with."

Eliza drops her head into her hands and grumbles, "I'm going to kill him." To her dad she says, "I'm never telling that bastard anything ever again. When the hell did Zeke have time to tell you?"

"On his way to the stadium," Jeremiah replies. "In his pregame call to me."

I don't know if they've forgotten I'm sitting here or not, but I'm enjoying this. I'm glad to know that Eliza's Instagram wasn't a lie about who she is because too often people put up an internet persona that doesn't match their real selves.

Eliza turns to look at me and gives me a look that I'm not quite able to read before she turns back to her dad.

"Of course he did," she says. "Can't have anything for myself in this family. Remind me to change my locks."

I let out a laugh. I don't mean to, but it just slips out. But it does cause Eliza to turn towards me with a smile on her face.

Jake comes over at that moment, clapping me on the shoulder and says, "Come on man, they just put out the food."

I stand up and glance over my shoulder to see Eliza talking to her dad again about something, but I can't hear what it is.

Jake leads me over to the food tables and I ask nodding towards the Foxes, "Do you know them."

He looks over to where I was nodding my head and reads the back of their jerseys.

"Oh yeah," he replies. "The Foxes. Zeke Fox plays tight end. He's tight with my buddy that always hooks me up with these seats."

"So, you know them well enough?" I ask.

"Never really had a conversation with either, why?"

"Oh, I just saw her at the game last night," I try replying nonchalantly.

Jake stops and looks at me with a mischievous glint to his eyes.

"Oh, so she's what caught your attention in the second yesterday."

I don't think I'm going to be able to get out of this, but I also don't want to say anything.

Apparently, that is all the confirmation that he needs because he sets his plate down and starts towards Eliza and Jeremiah. Not knowing what is about to happen, I follow Jake.

"What are you doing?" I hiss at him.

"Just trust me," he replies.

That's the thing, I don't know if I trust him. Sure, I trust him on the ice, but that's different. Outside of hockey, I barely know the guy.

Sliding in next to Eliza he says, "So I hear you're the pretty thing that caught Ratatouille's attention last night."

I slap him upside the head and Eliza turns toward Jake.

"You idiot," I hiss. "She's not a 'pretty thing,' she's a beautiful woman."

I realize that Eliza heard me when I see her cheeks start to turn pink.

Thankfully she ignores the comment and asks, "Ratatouille?"

Now it is my turn to turn pink. It's not that I hate the nickname, it's just I've never had a woman call me by it.

She quips, "I wasn't aware that there were any chefs being controlled by a rat around."

Her eyes only leave mine when Jake starts to explain, "Yep, he's our Remy."

Fucking hell man, I'm going to die in the presence of this woman without ever knowing what she tastes like.

"Oh, trust me, I'm very familiar with the movie *Ratatouille*," she replies. "But this feels very *How I Met Your Mother*-ish."

I look at her to see her smiling. Fuck, I want to make her smile more.

Jake seems confused when he asks, "What?"

"You know in *How I Met Your Mother* Barney is always playing wingman for Ted? 'Have you met Ted?'"

I let out a laugh. Of course, she is able to reference tv shows and movies like it's nothing.

Jake looks more confused and glances between me and Eliza as if we are sharing an inside joke.

Eliza beats me to the punch by saying, "Look if you're going to wingman maybe you should catch up on the reference before trying to pull a Barney Stintson. Or you know you can be the kind of wingman Goose is in *Top Gun*."

I watch as Jake's jaw drops, and let me tell you, I'm already fucked when it comes to this woman.

I'm about to say something when the announcer comes over the speakers. I take that as my cue to shut the fuck up and not bother Eliza for the moment.

CHAPTER 9
ELIZA

I can't really focus on Zeke's game; I'm too caught up in replaying the interaction with Remy's teammate.

During halftime I make my way to the restroom and on my way out I run into a solid mass of muscle. Looking up I find Remy looking down at me, smiling. Now I'm not short in any capacity—I'm actually above average height, well 5'10 might actually be considered tall—but damn he's tall.

Gesturing with my head I silently ask him to follow me, and to my surprise he does.

"Hi," I say breaking the silence between us.

"Hi," he replies, still smiling. "You're not getting shy on m now, are you?"

"Fuck no. I'm just not sure that it's appropriate to tell a virtual stranger that they are even prettier up close."

His eyes twinkle before replying, "Oh so you think I'm pretty?"

I stop in one of the halls between the boxes and turn to look at him.

"You don't need a bigger head," I reply, smiling.

He takes a step in my space and tells me, "I'm glad I ran into you."

I can see in his eyes that he is being genuine.

"You don't even know me," I hear myself respond.

"And I would like to change that." I can't help but stare at his lips as he says that.

I glance back up to his eyes and find him staring at my lips.

He takes another step closer and tucks a curl behind my ear before leaning his hand on the wall behind me. I have to work very hard not to swoon over the gesture; it's something that fictional men would do. He is now close enough that I can smell the woodsy tones lingering on him.

A shiver runs down my spine.

"Let me take you on a date," he practically whispers.

"How do you know I'm not some puck bunny trying to get with you because you're a hockey player?" I ask instead of just agreeing.

He gives me a smile before responding, "Baby I could tell you weren't a fucking puck bunny from the way you were watching the game more than the players. And you're not actively throwing yourself at me. Plus it seems you grew up in a sports household."

Another shiver runs down my spine.

"Let me take you out on a date," he says again running his fingers down my arm.

"What? You don't want to just fall into bed and see if we can just fuck it out of systems?"

"Trust me, I'd love nothing more than to do exactly that. But something tells me that one time won't ever be enough with you."

What the hell is happening? I'm not the kind of person to just fall for a guy with a pretty face that uses pretty words.

"So, what do you say?" Remy asks me.

"I'll give you one date to prove yourself," I reply already knowing it won't be just one.

"You drive a hard bargain. I'll text you the details."

I say, "DM."

I want to slap myself.

"Hm?"

"Since you don't have my number, you'll have to DM me."

"Any chance you'll be willing to cut me some slack and give me your number?"

I shake my head and reply, "Nope. You'll have to work for it."

"Figures," he says before walking off, leaving me standing there.

What the actual fuck just happened?

By the time I get back to my seat the third quarter is starting. I don't pay attention. I can't with the interaction I'd had with Remy playing on repeat in my head.

By the end of the game, I am ready to get out of here and go home, but I still have to see my brother.

I know I'm in for it when Zeke finds us in the family room.

"What's wrong with you, Liz?" Zeke asks me as he gives me a hug.

"Nothing," I reply, the lie blatantly obvious.

"I'm pretty sure she's still reeling from talking to that guy you were telling me about," my dad says before Zeke can say anything.

I'm going to die, and it will be my dad and brother's fault.

Zeke whips his head toward me, and asks, "What guy?"

"The hockey one," my dad replies, the traitor that he is.

Zeke's eyes widen and he starts bouncing on his toes.

"He was here? And you actually got to talk to him face to face?" Zeke asks, excitement very evident in his voice.

I turn around to leave saying over my shoulder, "Bye. I'll see y'all at Christmas."

Zeke grabs my arm before I can go anywhere, and I roll my eyes.

I both hate and love that my brother is my best friend.

"Please?" he asks me with puppy dog eyes.

I sigh. "Fine. But I really wish that you would learn some fucking boundaries."

"No you don't."

I huff.

"I talked to him for maybe five minutes. There's nothing more to it," I reply.

Zeke looks at our dad and says, "She did talk to him for less than five minutes but even I could feel the connection between them. Saw it with my own two eyes as well."

"Traitor," I say. "Y'all act like I've never brought a guy home or really even talked to one."

Zeke replies, "Well to be fair you haven't brought anyone home since you were dating Xander."

That was three years ago, and there's a reason he's my ex.

I give him a dead stare and say, "Y'all are worse than a bunch of girls."

Zeke throws his arms around my shoulders and replies, "It's cause we love and care for you, Lizzie."

I just shake my head and pat his back.

"Can we get the fuck out of here?" I ask when Zeke finally lets go.

"Fuck yes!" he exclaims, leading us out.

CHAPTER 10
REMINGTON

ME

I have to ask you something before I take you out

ELIZA

Very ominous

ME

You don't have a boyfriend, right?

ELIZA

No I don't have a boyfriend

ME

What about that guy you were with the other night at my game?

ELIZA

A little jealous are we?

Fuck. I've only had two conversations with her, but I can already picture the snarky tone she would use.

And yeah I'm man enough to admit to myself that I am a little jealous, but not man enough to admit that to her.

ELIZA

He's the director that I've been working with and invited him to the game to celebrate his film moving on to the next stage.

I sigh in relief and Krypto touches his paw to my face. Rubbing his head I say, "I'm okay buddy."

ME

So I don't have to worry about any boys lining up for you?

ELIZA

My milkshake brings all the boys to the yard

I let out a sharp laugh.

ME

Any exes to worry about?

ELIZA

Oh yeah you're going to have to defeat my seven evil exes.

I am stunned. This woman just made a *Scott Pilgram vs the World* reference. I've yet to meet someone that has seen that movie or even enjoyed it.

ELIZA

The boy was too stunned to speak

ME

Damn right I am

ELIZA

I look at Krypto and say, "Buddy I think I'm royally fucked when it comes to this girl already."

I also think I might already be halfway in love with Eliza.

I'm about to respond to Eliza when Georgia FaceTime's me.

"How's my favorite person?" I ask.

Georgia laughs and replies, "Max is great. Aren't you buddy."

She turns her phone so I can see my nephew.

"Hey Maxie," I say to him. "How's my favorite guy?"

Instantly a huge grin takes over his face and he starts to say, "Rex!"

"I miss you bud," I reply. "I'll see you soon, okay?"

Georgia turns the phone back to her and says, "Sooner rather than later this time okay Nash? You have no excuse now that you live closer."

I nod and reply, "I promise."

"You better because Max will hold you to your word," she threatens.

A smile breaks across my face, "I could never say no to him."

"I know, that's why I have no problem using him against you."

I laugh. Only my baby sister would use her son as leverage against me.

"So, what's new with you?" she asks casually, but I know she's trying to dig.

I tell her everything that's going on except for whatever the hell is happening with Eliza, because I want to hold off on my sisters finding out about her as long as possible.

Georgia starts to say something but a DM notification from Eliza pulls my attention.

> She shoots, she scores, and the crowd is…
> nowhere to be seen

"What's with the look on your face?" Georgia asks.

"What do you mean?" I reply. "I don't have a look on my face."

"Mmhm. Yeah okay. You definitely didn't have the look of some lovesick puppy."

"No I didn't."

"Oh my god. There's a girl, isn't there?"

Georgia's eyes grow two times the size.

"What? No." Even I can hear the crack in my voice.

"There is!" she exclaims. "Hold on."

Next thing I know she's added my younger sister, Arizona, to the call.

I hold back a groan as Ari asks, "What's up."

Georgia answers, "Nash was just about to tell me about his girl."

"She's not my girl," I reply without thinking. *Yet. Eliza isn't my girl yet.*

"Ha!" Georgia exclaims. "I knew that there was a girl!"

"Nashy has a girl?" Arizona asks in a sing songy voice.

I groan. I walked right into the trap without even seeing it. I could seriously smack myself for that.

Don't get me wrong, I love my sisters, I do. But holy fucking shit they are some of the nosiest people I know, and they meddle in my life like theirs depends on it.

"Fucking hell," I mutter.

Georgia is quick to reprimand me by saying, "Now Nash, there are young ears present."

"You might want to cover his ears then," I reply.

I don't think I can get through this conversation sober without dropping a few f-bombs.

"Come on Nash," Ari says. "Enlighten us on this girl you may or may not have."

Both of my sisters are smiling at me expectantly.

I debate the best way to get out of this conversation, but I know they won't drop it no matter how much I beg.

I'm almost thirty years old and somehow my two sisters always find a way to make me beg.

I run a hand down my face and say, "Both of you owe me big fucking time."

Their smiles widen knowing they had just won.

"Saw her at a game a couple of nights ago and we've had a couple of conversations," I say truthfully, even if it's not the full truth.

Georgia narrows her eyes slightly and asks, "What's her name?"

"Eliza," I reply, purposefully leaving out her last name. I know my sisters and I know they'll stalk Eliza on Instagram if given the chance.

"What's her last name?" Georgia asks.

Before I can say anything Arizona replies, "Fox. Her name is Eliza Fox."

My jaw drops. "How the fuck?"

Arizona shrugs and says, "She's the only Eliza that you follow."

"What the fuck?"

My question goes unanswered, but I'm honestly a little scared to find out how Arizona found out what Eliza's last name is.

"Oh my god!" Georgia practically squeals. "You already follow her?"

"She followed me, so I followed back," I say as if it's nothing.

"Ari," Georgia asks. "You know what this means?"

Arizona smirks and replies, "Our big brother is royally fucked over a girl he just met, Gigi."

"He's going to fall in love and be so fucking whipped for this girl," Georgia says.

"Wait till you see her," Arizona replies. "I'll send you her profile."

I don't think I can take this anymore.

"All right," I say abruptly. "Bye."

I hang up before I can hear anything else from them, and I just know they're going to tell our mom. In turn mom will call me and ask about Eliza.

Resting my phone on my chest I take in a deep breath before picking it back up to respond to Eliza.

ME

Please tell me you have an annoying sister

It's only after I hit send that I realize what I just did.

ELIZA

No. But I have an annoying twin brother. Why?

ME

Does he like prying into your life?

I smack my head. I know the answer to that, I'd overheard Eliza talking about it to her dad.

ELIZA

All the fucking time

ME

Glad it's not just me

ELIZA

You have a meddling sister?

ME

Two. Both are younger

ELIZA

Shit. As a younger sister myself I'll say sorry

ME

Don't be surprised if a Georgia and Arizona randomly start following you

ELIZA

They already know about me?

ME

Georgia apparently saw some kind of look on my face when you DMed me while I was FaceTiming her a few minutes ago

ELIZA

Let me guess she immediately clocked you and put your other sister on the call to drag it out of you

ME

Bingo. How'd you know?

ELIZA

Zeke basically did the same to me

Well he saw your notification on my phone and sat on me until I told him

ME

ELIZA

Just be glad you didn't have to share a womb with either of your sisters, Miller

Damn, she's got me there.

ME

I have to get ready to head to the arena.

Fuck. That did all kinds of things to me.

CHAPTER 11
ELIZA

Remy was right about his sisters following me on Instagram, I just hadn't expected them to do it so soon. I make a mental note to ask him if they've done this for every girl he's had an interest in.

I don't really mind them following me because it gives *me* a chance to stalk *them* and follow them back. It also means that I have something to keep my mind off of seeing him at the game.

That night when I walk into the arena I take a minute to take everything in. I love the smell of the arena, the chill of the ice, and the sound of players on the ice.

About halfway to my seat I feel my phone buzzing in my pocket. Pulling it out I see that Quincy, one of the directors I work with a lot, calling me. This isn't anything unusual, I'm just surprised he is calling me after 5 o'clock. He tends to make work calls during the middle of the day unless he is on a night shoot. And we also don't really talk outside of work, so a personal call would be kind of weird.

Answering I say, "Hi Quince, what's up?"

"Question," he responds. "Have you wrapped your latest project yet?"

Getting to my seat I answer, "Picture locked a couple of days ago."

I can hear the smile in his voice as he says, "Oh thank god. I thought I was going to have to pry you out of Brian's hands."

I smile and reply, "Quincy, you're the one who recommended me to Brian. So you really only have yourself to blame."

Just then both teams start to come out of the tunnels for warmups, and the crowd so far cheers for the Flames.

"It's not my fault you're so fucking good at your job," he says.

I let out a laugh.

I've known Quincy since our last year at film school, so he's been able to watch my style be defined over the past few years, and in turn I've seen him flourish as an up-and-coming director.

"Am I interrupting anything?" Quincy asks, likely picking up on the arena noise.

"No," I reply. "Just waiting on a hockey game to start."

"Okay good, because I want to run something by you, and it's totally okay if you say no."

I roll my eyes, even though he can't see.

About that time Remy comes up to the glass in front of me, and smiles at me. I smile back and he motions for me to come down.

I'm starting down the stairs when Quincy says, "Okay so I'm working on finishing the script for my next project."

"As one does," I reply, because he doesn't just direct, he also writes most of his scripts.

Quincy continues, "So that means that preproduction will start soon and production a few months after that."

I assume he's already been greenlit, otherwise we likely wouldn't be having this conversation.

I nod and ask, "You want me as editor?"

"Yes, but that's not what I want to run by you."

I look up at Remy and he mouths *Hi* to me.

I mouth back *Hi* to him and he holds up a finger to tell me to wait a minute before skating away. I have no idea what he's doing but I wait anyways.

At that moment Quincy asks, "How do you feel about getting flown out to Scotland and editing the dailies while one set?"

It takes me a second to register what he just asked.

Remy skates back over to me and tosses a puck over the glass. I catch it and stare at the writing on it. I assume it's Remy's handwriting, but the little blocky letters don't really tell me anything other than:

meet me in the tunnels after the game?

I read it again just to make sure I read it right the first time. I look up to find him staring at me expectantly.

I'm double shocked for two different reasons, and my brain seems to be short circuiting a little.

"Liz, you there?" Quincy asks through my phone.

"Yeah, give me a sec," I reply.

I look at Remy and mouth, *Seriously?*

He nods.

I hold up the puck and mouth, *Is this your grand gesture?*

He lets out a laugh, and shrugs.

I shake my head and mouth, *Yes.*

He gives an excited fist pump with one of his hands bringing it towards his stomach. I can't help the small laugh that comes out.

"Eliza," Quincy says, reminding me that I am still on the phone with him.

Without letting my smile drop I reply, "You're asking me if I want to pull a *Baby Driver?*"

"Yes!" he exclaims.

Remy stands there staring at me as if he is trying to figure out what I am saying. For some reason I don't mind.

I bring my free hand up to pinch the bridge of my nose as I

reply, "This is literally most editors worst fear, but yet it's some's biggest dream."

My eye lock with Remy's and I can feel a calm settling over me.

"I know, and you don't have to give me an answer tonight," Quincy replies. "You still have a few months. And even if you say no I'd still like to fly you out during shooting."

My jaw drops and Remy quirks an eyebrow at me.

"Are you serious?" I ask.

"Deadly," Quincy replies. "You've done so much for me behind the scenes, so I think you deserve this."

"Wow."

"Look, I'll let you think on it, but call or text me in the next couple of weeks so I can tell Cass, and she'll email you official stuff when we get into preproduction."

"Yeah, okay."

With that Quincy hangs up the phone and I run a hand through my hair; Remy watching my movements.

You good? he mouths.

I nod.

Someone on the ice gets his attention, and he sharply nods.

Looking back at me he mouths, *Later?*

I nod again and watch as he skates away.

"Believe it or not there is genuinely something between you two," my dad says as I make my back up to my seat.

Tucking the puck into my pocket I reply, "I didn't know if you were coming or not, old man."

"Who are you calling old?" he fakes hurt. "Nice subject change by the way."

Well, I learned from the best, but I'm not telling him that, instead I just roll my eyes and ask, "Can we just not talk about it?"

Dad throws up his hands in surrender and replies, "Fine, but no promises when your brother finds out."

It isn't an if, it is a when, because knowing my father he will likely tell Zeke. There are zero secrets between the three of us, simply because none of us can keep our mouths shut. I just wish that my dad and brother weren't witnesses to this potential relationship I have with Remy as it unfolds in real time.

Lucky for me my dad stays true to his word, and we don't talk about mine and Remy's interaction the entire game. I will just have to prepare myself for when Zeke finds out.

CHAPTER 12
REMINGTON

don't know who Eliza had been on the phone with when I tossed her that puck, but I didn't like the way they made her face twist the way it did. The whole game I couldn't get that fucking image out of my head for more than a few seconds. It doesn't matter, I still played my game how I always do, and I will find out in a few minutes when I talk to her

I can't get off the ice fast enough, but I also have to play it cool so none of my teammates start asking questions. I love my teammates, but holy shit they are some nosey fuckers when they want to be. It probably also doesn't help that in the few months they've known me I've barely given a woman more than a one-night stand. So, me actively trying to talk to one for more than just a hook up will probably blow their fucking minds.

As quickly as I can without drawing attention, I shower and get dressed.

Fuck, I think as some of the guys start to file out of the locker room. *I didn't tell Eliza where exactly to find me.*

I'm about to pull out my phone to DM her when I hear, "I'm so glad I had an idea of where to go, because I sure as hell ain't psychic."

A huge grin breaks out over my face from not only hearing

Eliza, but also hearing her southern accent coming out a bit stronger than normal. I turn to look at her, and my smile grows wider, if that's even possible.

Without thinking I jog over to her and warp her up in a big hug.

Tentatively she wraps her arms around me, and I bury my face in the crook of her neck. Taking in a deep breath I can smell the arena on her, but also something that I'm sure is distinctly Eliza.

Pressed against my chest, she says, "Not that I'm complaining about a 6'5 right winger giving me one of the best hugs I've ever had, but I didn't think that we were at this stage in our relationship."

I smile at the knowledge that she probably looked up my stats to know that.

"Sorry," I reply letting her go. "I wasn't thinking."

She shrugs.

"There is more than flirty banter between us, right?" she asks and almost sounds a little insecure.

I trail my hands down her arms and reply, "I don't think I can be just one and done with you, and I barely fucking know you."

She smiles at that. I can tell that she appreciates the conformation about feeling the same way she is likely feeling.

"Great game today, Ratatouille," Grant Sanders, the captain for the Flames calls out.

"You too cap," I reply.

He locks eyes with Eliza and a mischievous glimmer appears in his eyes. I sometimes can't tell he if he is worse or if Jake Smith is.

"And who do we have here?" he asks coming toward us instead of going towards the player parking lot.

Internally I groan, because of fucking course this is happening to me of all people.

"Cap this is Eliza," I reply, hoping that he won't make a big deal out of this but I really should know better.

Grant holds out his hand to Eliza and she takes it.

"So, you're the woman who has captured the attention of out Ratatouille," Grant says.

Eliza laughs and replies, "You know Smith said something very similar to me the other day." She turns to me. "Do you have a problem getting girls? Is that why they're acting like I'm some anomaly?"

Before I say anything, Grant says, "In the few months he's been here he's not shown any interest in anyone long term or had anyone to wear his jersey."

I look at the number on her sleeve to see a big lime green #26 on it. Stepping behind Eliza I move her hair out of the way to see Ramirez at the top rather than Miller. It's the same jersey she'd been wearing that first day I saw her.

"Don't you have any other jerseys?" I ask, barely containing my growl.

She looks over her shoulder to look at the back of her jersey and asks, "What's wrong with my jersey?"

"It has another man's last name on it," I reply.

Grant lets out a laugh and moves to see what I'm talking about.

"And?" Eliza asks turning to face us. "I saw my first hockey game the night he got his first career shutout. And Zeke always says that #26 is our lucky number."

Grant opens his mouth to ask but I answer, "Her twin brother."

He nods, satisfied with that answer. Grant should know better than to think I would steal another man's girl.

I can see the humor in his eyes as I say, "We're going to have to fix that. Can't have you wearing another man's name."

I can see the challenge in Eliza's eyes as she replies, "Jealous? Cause you can't be jealous over something that's not yours."

Grant says, "I'm gonna leave you two to this. See you later Ratatouille. Nice to meet you, Eliza. It's clear Remy has his hands full with you."

With that he leaves—as if he's not the one that opened that can of worms—leaving just me and Eliza alone in the hall.

"We're going to revisit the jersey thing later," I tell her. "But do you want to get something to eat?"

"Is this your one date?" she asks in return.

"No," I reply. "This is just two people getting some food."

"Uh huh. Okay. Where were you thinking?"

"You know that diner on Peachtree boulevard?" She nods. "I was kinda thinking there."

"Okay, I'll meet you there."

Before I can say anything, she turns around and starts walking toward the exit that will presumably take her to her car.

Fuck. I had hoped that we'd ride together. But I guess it makes more sense for us to drive separately, that way her car doesn't get locked in here.

And fuck I didn't get to find out who she'd been on the phone with, but I'm going to make sure that I do at the diner.

CHAPTER 13
ELIZA

'm not going to lie, I'm a little freaked out. First Remy hugs me like we've known each other for ages, and then he got jealous that I was wearing another man's jersey.

Like I know we are moving fast, but I didn't think we were going supersonic.

Before pulling into the diner, I take a deep breath. Everything is going to be fine, just a-okay.

Remy is standing against the diner wall waiting on me as I park. I give him a smile and hope to high heaven that he won't pick up on how fucking freaked out I am.

We haven't even gone on a date or anything yet for crying out loud.

"I have a question for you," Remy says as I get out of my Jeep.

"It's not a marriage proposal, is it?" I joke. "Because I think it's too soon."

He lets out a laugh and opens the diner door for me.

"No," he says as we are led to a table. "Who were you on the phone with that caused you to have that look on your face?"

That's not what I thought he was going to ask. To be fair I wasn't really sure what I thought he was going to ask. I also didn't realize that I'd had a certain look on my face. Though I shouldn't be surprised, because he had been standing right there during that part of the conversation.

"Oh, one of the directors that I work with a lot was running something by me about his next project," I reply.

Remy raises an eyebrow and asks, "Is that all?"

I kind of hate that he can already read me with relative ease.

I sigh and say, "He wanted to know if I was willing to pull a *Baby Driver.*"

Remy gives me a questioning look.

I drop my head into my hands and explain, "Sorry I'm so used to speaking to other film people when talking about this kind of stuff, I forget that not everyone understands. If I ever say something you don't understand, please just ask me to explain it."

He laughs and asks, "What do you mean by pulling a *Baby Driver?*"

"Okay, so, when they were filming *Baby Driver,* they had the editor on set editing the film from the dailies. Which is pretty much the raw unedited footage from the day."

"And is that bad?" he asks, seeming genuinely curious.

"Some editors like editing that way," I answer as I start to mess with a napkin. "But most think it's a shitty way to edit a film. See I personally like having all of the footage in front of me so I can see where it's going."

Realization dawns on Remy's face.

"I just realized you edit movies," he says sitting back in shock. "Like I saw the tag in your bio on Instagram but didn't think anything of it. All the film posters in your film highlight makes a lot more sense now."

"Bit of a stalker, aren't you?" I tease.

"So you worked on all of those movies?"

I nod and start tearing the napkin. "Yeah."

"Holy shit! That's so fucking awesome."

I smile at that.

Not many of the guys I've gotten with in the past would've said that. Most of them just wanted to know which actors I'd worked with or if I'd hooked up with any famous people.

Remy's eyes widen even more, and he exclaims, "Holy shit! You worked on *Down Comes Night*, didn't you?"

"Yeah, I was the lead editor," I reply.

"Oh my god! That's my favorite movie that's come out in the past few years."

"My friend, Athena, was the director. It was her passion project, and she trusted me to put it all together."

I take a sip of my Coke as I watch Remy's face.

Down Comes Night isn't a blockbuster by any means—it's more indie than anything—and I've met very few people that have found it organically, not to say there aren't more out there. I'm just glad that Athena's film is getting the recognition it deserves.

I pull out my phone to text her about this, ignoring basic date etiquette.

ME

The guy that I'm into says that his favorite movie from recent years is DCN

ATHENA GODDESS OF WISDOM

HOLY FUCKING CRAP!! Are you joking?

ME

Not at all

ATHENA GODDESS OF WISDOM

OH MY GOD!!

That has literally made my night. I think I might cry from joy!

I set my phone on the table and spin it toward Remy so he can see.

"So, I'm a guy you're into?" he asks after he reads the messages.

"Is that all you got out of that?" I return.

"No," he replies. "But it's nice to know you can talk to your friends about me."

I roll my eyes at his smug grin.

"Will she really cry?" he asks with a hint of worry.

"Honestly I have no idea," I reply. "She's a bit dramatic so it's really a toss-up. But if she does, just know it's cause she's so happy to hear someone liked her film enough to deem it one of their favorites."

He smiles and nods.

"But just know, now that she knows I'm interested in a guy, my girls group chat will likely be blowing up," I say.

His smile widens, and why does it make him so much more attractive?

"Speaking of favorites," he segways. "What's your favorite movie?"

"This feels like it's creeping into date territory," I joke.

He holds his hands up and says, "I'm just asking a question so I can gauge if this can continue or not."

I shake my head, trying to hold back my laugh.

Our waitress sets down our food.

"*Back to the Future*," I finally say. "It's been my favorite movie since I was like three."

Remy nods and replies, "Classic. This can continue."

I laugh and ask, "What about you? What's your all-time favorite film?"

He thinks on it for a moment, tapping his chin, before saying, "Probably *Cars*."

"Nice," I say. "Love that movie. My dad has a buddy that likes making movie props and has a Lightning McQueen car. Makes my day anytime I'm in Oakwood and see it."

Remy's jaw drops and he replies, "That is so fucking awesome! That would make my day too!"

We continue talking, even long after our food is gone. When we finally get up to leave, I'm almost sad that the night is ending. I'm half tempted to invite Remy back to my place so we can keep things going, but I ultimately decide against it.

We say our goodbyes and get into our respective vehicles. I'm about to pull out of my parking spot when a notification comes through on my phone.

REMINGTON

How are you at bowling?

ME

I'm a pro at it on the Wii.

REMINGTON

Do those skills translate to real life?

ME

They say you're either good at bowling or good in bed

REMINGTON

. That doesn't answer my question

ME

. Why?

REMINGTON

Just trying to get some ideas to plan our date

ME

Well chop chop hockey guy. We're not getting younger

REMINGTON

Don't rush me woman. You can't rush perfection.

ME

Rome wasn't built in a day

REMINGTON

Exactly. I'll let you know when I've got it solidified.

But it will likely be after this stretch of road games.

ME

Can't wait for the games to be on everything else but ESPN+. Like that's what I fucking pay for.

REMINGTON

You win some you lose some.

I smile at that.

ME

Well goodnight, Remington Miller

REMINGTON

Goodnight, Eliza Fox.

I put my phone down and head home. The entire drive home, there is a smile on my face because of this hockey player who has likely already stolen my heart without even realizing it.

CHAPTER 14
REMINGTON

read Eliza's message as I get to my seat on the plane and let out a groan.

I let out a laugh, which earns me a look from one of our third line defensemen. I give him a sheepish look and turn back to my phone.

I shake my head. I don't know how this woman already affects me so much, but she does. I can't tell her that yet, because one we barely know each other and two this could lead to nothing. I don't fucking want it to lead to nothing, but I also have to think realistically about this.

ME

You're right. I'm sorry. The female gender is far superior.

ELIZA

Thank you for agreeing.

I'm honestly kinda surprised that Zeke hasn't done that to you

ME

I'm afraid to ask if he would

ELIZA

I love him, but the fucker has literally no boundaries when it comes to me

ME

ELIZA

But don't let him fool you, he's just a big teddy bear.

ME

Phew.

ELIZA

He's also lucky I have to love him

ME

Out of the corner of my eye I see the flight attendants getting in position to give us the safety talk.

ME

We're about to take off, but I'll talk to you later?

ELIZA

Talk to you later Remy

I smile and put my phone down.

"Dude you are so totally fucked," Grant says standing over my shoulder in the seat behind me.

"Jesus," I startle. "Give a guy a heart attack why don't you?"

He raises an eyebrow at me and replies, "You're still fucked."

I sigh and pinch the bridge of my nose.

"I don't even know her," I say, which is only half a lie.

Grant isn't fazed as he replies, "Sometimes the best ones start as strangers."

He claps me on the shoulder and gets to his seat.

Jake comes up next to me and I scoot over. He daps me up before sitting down.

"Cap knows." I practically whisper to him.

He looks at me and asks, "Knows what?"

"About Eliza," I reply. "I don't know, he saw me talking to her after our last game, and I didn't know what to do so I introduced her to him."

I take a deep breath, only now realizing that I'm rambling and dumping all of this on him.

"In the time I've known you, you have not given two shits about a woman, so this is a nice change," he says through a smile.

I groan. "I swear if you or Grant say anything about this to any of the other guys I'll murder both of you."

"Even Misha and Axel?" he asks.

"Even them."

Jake mimes zipping his lips. "My lips are sealed. I can't speak for Cap, but I can speak for myself."

I relax a little and reply, "Thank you."

"He totally freaked the fuck out over her wearing another man's jersey," Grant says out of nowhere.

"Jesus Christ, cap," I say. "You can't keep doing that."

"Are you talking about her wearing her brother's jersey?" Jake asks, and I truly want to die.

This is hell, it has to be. I'm being punished for something the universe deems punishable and this is my seventh circle of hell.

"No," I grit. "That doesn't count since it's not only her brother's name plastered across her back, but also hers."

"She was wearing Ramirez's jersey," Grant supplies seeming very proud of himself with his arms draped over the back of our seats.

Jake's jaw drops.

"I'm going to kill both of you," I say.

Grant explains, "To be fair I thought it was Ratatouille's because all I could see was the number."

Jake nods and replies, "Understandable."

"This must be my own personal hell," I mutter.

Jake pats me on the shoulder and says, "There, there Remy, everything will be alright."

"I hate you both."

This stretch of road games is going to be torture for two reasons now: Grant and Jake are totally going to torture the fuck out of me, likely roping Misha and Axel into this, and it will be a few days before I'll be able to see Eliza again.

I know I haven't known Eliza all that long, but I do enjoy spending time with her. Even though we've barely spent any time with together, just from the few times we have spent together I can tell that something about her just draws me to her.

I hold back a groan. I honestly can't get away from these fuckers quick enough. It really sucks that I'm forced to be on a plane with them for the next couple of hours.

Even though I'm feeling like I'm in one of the nine circles of hell, I never had this kind of camaraderie with my old team. And I have to say I feel like these guys genuinely care about me, and that I actually fit in with them. My old teammates were friendly, but I never truly felt like one of them, even though I played with them for a good portion of my career. So this is really nice.

CHAPTER 15
ELIZA

"**G**irl, you have got to tell me about this guy," Athena says as I answer my phone.

"Well hello to you too," I reply.

"Liza," she says. "You wouldn't have told me you were into him if you didn't think there was anything to it."

I sigh. I know I'm not going to get out of this, but I can still try. I'm honestly just glad that our friend Cam hasn't been roped into this yet. It's not like I don't want to talk about Remy, it's just I'm not really ready to tell people about him yet. I think most of that has to do with I have no fucking clue where this thing is going, and I'm used to relationships having a certain order when starting out.

"I barely know him," I say truthfully. "And we haven't been on a true date."

"Yet," Athena replies. "And don't lie to me. I can hear the smile in your voice from talking about him."

I glance away from my phone and try to suppress my smile with no success.

"And now you're smiling even more because you were trying to stop."

Fuck. Sometimes I hated how she knew me so well. I guess that's what happens with a best friend.

I take a deep breath and tell her everything. When I tell her about the puck he threw me, she squeals, and I have to brace myself for her reaction to his hug.

"Oh, my fucking god!" she exclaims. "He barely knows you and gave you that kind of hug?"

"Yeah," I reply as I stare off at the puck sitting on my mantle. I mentally make a note to get a special case for it.

"My god Liz," Athena says. "You're living something out of a fucking rom-com."

I throw my head back and reply, "I know, tell me about it. And I think I might be so totally fucked for him. Like halfway in love with him fucked."

"Hell, yeah you are," Athena encourages. "Do you know what he's going to do for your first date?"

"Technically our second," I say, forgetting I haven't told her the rest of the story.

"Um excuse me? Eliza Grace Fox are you holding back on me?"

I let out a laugh. "No. We just got sidetracked after the hug part."

I tell her how I let him take me to the diner after his game and how I insisted that it wasn't a date but deep down I knew it actually was.

"Oh my god," Athena says once I'm finally done. "You weren't even this serious about Xander and you were with him for two years."

She's the second person to mention my ex. Which okay I understand, he was my last real boyfriend, but still there's a reason we broke up. Call it creative differences if you will. I could quote "Cell Block Tango" but I'm not going to, not entirely at least.

"I know," I whine. "Thena what am I supposed to do?"

"Go on a date with the guy, duh," she says. "Has he mentioned anything about it?"

"He asked me how I was at bowling and that he was trying to get some feelers. Then said it would likely be after his stretch of road games. And I still have to tell Cam."

"Don't worry about her right now," Athena replies. "You'll have to keep me updated on your date though. I love you but I have to run."

"Go be the famous director I know you'll be."

"I knew I kept you around for a reason."

I laugh and we hang up.

Looking at the time I see that it's almost for puck drop at Remy's game against the Anaheim Stars.

Debating on DMing him or not I decide to just go for it.

ME

Good luck Remy

REMINGTON

You watching?

ME

It's actually on ESPN+, so yes

Plus it's only 10 here

REMINGTON

Good. Keep an eye out for me when I score

I don't want to think about what he is implying, but I can still feel the blush creeping up my cheeks.

It isn't until halfway through the second period when Remy scores. I pull up the camera on my phone and face the camera towards me before hitting record. I don't know what is compelling me to do this, but I am.

The camera cuts to a close up on Remy, and he stares at the camera dead on as he mouths *That's for you Liz.*

My mouth drops open as my free hand flies up to my mouth. I can feel a blush creeping up my face.

On the tv they play a replay of his goal, and my eyes watch his movements.

One of the announcers says, "I wonder what he said after that goal."

The other replies, "I think the better question is, who is he saying it to? Because I believe that was one hundred percent directed at someone at home."

"Holy fucking hell," I say through a laugh. "The woman was too stunned to speak." I run a hand over my face. "Oh my god."

I stop the recording and don't think twice about sending it to him. If Remy wants to affect me like that, then it's only fair I do the same to him. Even though I know he won't see it until after the game, I still feel a bit of smug satisfaction.

CHAPTER 16
REMINGTON

Once I found out that Eliza would be watching the game, I made sure she would know that my first goal of the night would be for her.

When we headed back to the locker room for second intermission, I made the mistake of looking at my phone. I saw that I had a notification from Eliza, and I sure as hell wasn't going to open it in the locker room because I'm not sure what I'll find or what it will do to me.

After the game I'm antsy to get back to my hotel room to see what Eliza had sent.

Once I get in my room I quickly change and lay up against my headboard.

I'm surprised to see that she sent me a video. I click play.

Her focus is on her tv, but my focus is on her. Even if there wasn't volume, I would've known the exact moment I said the goal was for her. Her jaw drops and a blush starts creeping over her beautiful face.

"Fuck," I say throwing my head back as I feel my dick twitch.

I watch her eyes follow the replay, and I know I'm done for. I never thought seeing a woman watch me play would be attractive to me, but here we are.

One the screen she says, "Holy fucking hell."

And if I wasn't fully hard before, I am now.

Yanking my shorts and underwear down I give my cock two short but hard pumps before running my thumb over the tip, feeling the precum already there.

My head smacks the headboard as I throw it back.

I don't even try to stop myself from picturing Eliza's hands on me as she pumps up and down, with a small twist at the end.

I imagine one of her hands reaching down between her legs and flicking her clit before moving her lips to my tip.

She lightly kisses me before licking up the precum then licks the underside of my shaft.

My hips lift up and start snapping into my hand, and I know I'm not going to last much longer.

I imagine my hand is Eliza's mouth and she is looking up at me with those blueish gray eyes of hers with tears in her eyes as I fuck her mouth.

Another rough pump and I imagine that she is sucking my cock as I pump into her mouth. I imagine my cock hitting the back of her throat with each thrust.

"Swallow every last drop," I imagine saying to her as my movements become jerkier.

The imaginary Eliza bobs her head on my cock before I feel my release.

In my head I watch as she swallows every last bit just like I had told her to. She pops her mouth off my dick, and a trail of saliva hangs from her mouth to my softening dick.

I open my eyes, breathing heavy and see the mess I made. Come all over my stomach and hand.

Holy fucking shit. I've never come like that before, and I know it is all because of Eliza, even if she isn't actually here.

I quickly walk to the bathroom to clean myself up.

I bet the real Eliza feels ten times better, I think as I hop into the shower. *I'm ruined for any other woman, and I haven't even tasted her yet.*

After a quick shower I leave the bathroom to put on a clean pair of boxer briefs, and grab my phone.

The video is still pulled up when I unlock it and quickly return to our messages.

ME

You don't even want to know the mess I just made because of that video

Her response comes a few seconds later.

ELIZA

You going to paint me like one of your French girls with all the cum coming out of your body?

I don't even think twice about hitting the call button at the top of our DMs after reading her message.

"Holy fucking shit, Liza," I say the second it connects. "You're going to get me hard again in like record time."

She lets out a laugh and replies, "You know I was just messing with you, but thanks for confirming you were thinking about me while getting yourself off. Might add that to my own self-care time."

"Fucking Christ woman," I groan. "You're the reason I was in that position in the first place."

"You're welcome," she replies, and I swear I can hear the twinkle in her eyes. "Have you thought about me any other time?"

This woman, I swear.

"You're going to be the death of me and my dick, Eliza," I say instead of answering her question.

She laughs and replies, "I bet it's a nice dick, so we wouldn't want that now would we?"

"Is it weird if I say I miss you?"

She sighs and I mentally prepare for what she's about to say.

"No," she starts, and I can hear her moving around. "Because I weirdly miss you too."

"I think it's weird that I miss you more than my cat," I tell her.

I can tell her whole demeanor changes after I say that because I can her the excitement on her voice as she asks, "You have a cat?"

Putting her on speaker I send her a picture of Krypto curled up on my couch, passed out in the afternoon sunlight.

I reply, "Yeah, he's been with me the past two years."

When the picture goes through and she sees it she exclaims, "Oh my god! He's adorable. What's his name?"

"Krypto," I reply wishing I was able to see her reaction to seeing the picture of my cat, because I know it would've melted my heart.

Eliza gasps and asks, "Remington Miller, are you a closet nerd?"

I laugh and reply, "Possibly."

"You know I'm not going to make fun of you, so you can tell me the truth. It's not going to be like that episode of *Psych* where Freddie Prinze Jr. thinks his hot wife won't like him if he doesn't act like a meathead jock."

"How do I know I can trust you?" I ask teasing her, knowing full well that I can trust her even without really knowing her.

A moment later a picture comes through our message thread. I pick up my phone to see that Eliza sent me a picture of her and her dad with James Tolken. On one side her dad is dressed as Maverick from *Top Gun* and on the other she's dressed like Marty McFly from *Back to the Future*, which is so fucking cool.

Another picture comes through and it's Eliza in the same outfit, only this time she's with Micheal fucking J. Fox. My jaw hits the fucking floor.

She sends a few more pictures, and I don't think my jaw will ever come off the floor it's just permanently glued there now.

In one picture Eliza's dressed as Napolean Dynamite and her dad is dressed as Forrest Gump, and they are standing next to William Zabka and Ralph Machio.

In another Jeremiah is dressed as flight suit Maverick and Eliza has on wizarding robes while standing next to Chevy Chase.

And to drive it all home, the last picture is her dressed as a jedi standing next to Hayden fucking Christensen.

I eventually I am able to find my words and say, "Liza I was not aware of your game."

She laughs.

Looking at the pictures again I ask, "How the fuck does your dad look so much like Forrest Gump here?"

She laughs again and replies, "I don't know, but it's kind of scary."

"If you've never worn Leia's gold bikini, I might be adding it to my list of fantasies."

"Ah yes the sexiest and most sexist costume in all of *Star Wars* is every guy's wet dream," she says drily.

"You'd wear it in the bedroom for me and only me," I reply getting an urge of possessiveness.

"If I play into your fantasies," Eliza says unfazed. "Then you'll have to play into mine."

I groan and reply, "Death by combustion from the greatest orgasm ever, simply because a fucking hot girl is telling me sweet things."

"A kinky closet nerd," she says through a laugh. "Fucking hell Rem, why do you have to be exactly my type, but times ten?"

"I could be saying the same thing about you."

I turn on the hotel tv and turn the volume low. Flipping through the channels I land on the Food Network, hoping not to get another hard on.

"Did you name Krypto or was that already his name?" she asks, and I can hear her yawn.

I look at the time to see it's well past one in the morning, which means even later for her.

"I named him," I reply. "I've always liked Superman."

She hums and says, "I'm more of a Batman person, well really Red Hood, but you get the point. But don't get me wrong I do still like the boy scout, he helped get me back into DC. Though Battison is one of the best live action detective Batman's in my opinion."

"Battison?" I ask.

"Robert Pattison's Batman. It's a shame his Batman and David Corenswet's Superman will likely never meet."

"Why?"

I love hearing her talk, even about nerdy stuff like this.

"Because they are some of the most accurate representations we have so far, but there's no guarantee that James Gunn will hire Robert Pattison to play Batman in the DCU. Especially if it's said that his Batman is actually in the else worlds verse."

"I never thought of it like that," I say.

"Yeah, those are my thoughts on SuperBat. But if you ask me if I'm team Cap or team Iron Man, I'll say that you're wrong if you say anything other than team Cap."

"Trust me," I say "I'm team Cap all the way. Especially since he was right in the end."

"Good," Eliza yawns. "I knew you were a good one."

"Do you want me to hang up?" I ask after a few seconds, struggling to keep my eyes open.

"No," she replies sleepily. "If that's okay."

"More than okay, Liza."

Not long after I fall asleep. Even though Eliza's not next to me it's still one of the best nights of sleep I've had in a while. Which probably says a lot, so I can just imagine what it would be like with her actually next to me.

CHAPTER 17
ELIZA

It's been four days since Remy left for his away games. I know they have an off day before playing at home again, but I have no idea when the team, gets home or if I'll see Remy before his game. Honestly, I'm not even sure when their practices are.

I know I can just ask him, but I don't really want to because where's the fun in that. I like being on my toes a little.

I'm about to start making some lunch when Zeke bursts through my front door.

"Have you ever heard of knocking?" I ask as he barely gets the door closed.

"No time. Bout to shit myself," he replies taking off down the hall.

"At least go to the guest bath!" I yell after him.

I could've had a sister, but no the universe stuck me with my fucking brother.

I decide to go ahead and make some extra spaghetti for Zeke. Knowing him he'll be hungry, and I don't share food from my plate. He's learned that the hard way over the years.

When he finally comes out of the bathroom I ask, "Could you

not have held it until you got to your own fucking place, or wherever the hell you were going?"

He pulls out one of the bar stools and sits down as he replies, "No you were closest, and I was not going to risk shitting myself like a baby."

I roll my eyes and say, "Never trust a fart."

"Exactly!" he looks at the stove and asks, "What'ca making?"

"Spaghetti."

Zeke's eyes light up and before he can ask, I say, "Yes there's enough for you."

"You're the best sister a guy could ask for."

I look over at him to see him with his hands holding up his head as he sweetly blinks at me.

"I'm your only sister dipshit," I reply.

"Doesn't mean you aren't the best sister. You're also the only woman a man needs."

I know he's referring to our mom, but I don't say anything because neither of us have ever let her leaving affect us. At least I think that's the case, because I literally couldn't care less about the bitch.

A phone dings and Zeke pulls his out to check it.

"Not mine," he says.

"Can you check mine?" I ask. "It's on the couch."

He nods and gets up to retrieve my phone.

"Remington is messaging you," Zeke calls out. "You still haven't given him your number?"

"No," I reply. "I told him he had to work for it."

Zeke smiles and says, "That's my girl. Make 'em work for it."

I smile as I roll my eyes.

I'm about to tell Zeke that lunch is ready when my phone starts ringing.

I'm not quick enough to get it because Zeke snatches it up and answers before I can do anything.

"Hiya hockey daddy, how's it going?" Zeke asks as he pretends to twirl his hair, even it's too short.

I fake gag and try and grab my phone from him.

"Z, you bastard. Give me my phone back!" I exclaim.

He keeps dodging me—curse his stupid athletic body—before finally saying, "Eliza dear your man would like a word."

I snatch my phone from him, punch him in the stomach and grit, "Go eat your fucking lunch."

I head towards my bedroom so Zeke can't hear my conversation.

"I'm sorry about him," I say into my phone.

Remy chuckles before replying, "So about our date."

"You aren't canceling on me already, are you? If so, I'm blaming my fucking brother."

"No," he replies. "I would move mountains just to go on a date with you."

That makes me smile.

"Are you free tonight around six?" Remy asks me.

"Yeah," I reply. "Are you going to tell me what we're going to do?"

He hums before saying, "No, I think I'll keep that part a surprise. Just wear something comfortable."

"Can I make a guess?" I ask.

I can hear the smile in his voice as he replies, "Yes, but you're not likely to get it."

"The Georgia Aquarium," I say.

"Nope. I told you you wouldn't get it, but I will keep that in mind for next time."

"Someone's getting ahead of themselves."

"Confidence is key, Eliza."

I smile. "Well, I guess it's a date then."

Zeke lets out a loud whoop from the other side of my bedroom door.

"Fucking bastard," I mutter. "I might kill him. You'll be my alibi, right?"

Remy lets out a sharp laugh. "Right."

"Do you need me to send you my address?" I ask Remy.

"That would be great," he replies. "See you at six."

We hang up and I stand there for a minute before Zeke throws open my bedroom door holding a bowl of spaghetti.

"Okay I've waited long enough," he says slurping some noodles into his mouth. "Tell me everything."

I roll my eyes and sit down on my bed.

"Zeke," I say, and he turns serious.

One thing about my brother is he always knows when to joke with me and when he needs to be serious.

Placing a hand on my shoulder Zeke asks, "What's going on in that head of yours Liza?"

I wrap my arms around my stomach and reply, "I really like this guy, and I barely know him. But I'm also fucking scared of how fast things seem to be going."

"Hey," he taps under my chin to get me to look up at him. "He's not going to do anything you aren't comfortable with. He's probably feeling the same way you are, and that's the thing about feelings Eliza. They have a mind of their fucking own, and it's not always going to be rational when feelings are involved."

"When did you get wise?" I jokingly ask.

"Pft. I've always been like this."

I shake my head.

"Just be out of here before six," I say.

Zeke slaps a hand over his heart and fake gasps, "You mean I can't be here when you get picked up for your date? How am I supposed to gauge this guy for my baby sister?"

I narrow my eyes at him and reply, "I'm ten minutes younger than you, bastard."

"Still my baby sister," he says as he ruffles my hair and sprints away.

I don't even feel like chasing after him, I just stay on my bed for what feels like an eternity.

Eventually I get up to eat lunch and try not to freak the fuck out about tonight.

It's just a date, I think to myself. *I've been on plenty of dates in the past, this is no different.*

Psyching myself out doesn't really seem to help so I grab the book I' m currently reading and get comfy on my couch.

Fiction always makes things better.

CHAPTER 18
ELIZA

At 5:55 there is a knock on my front door. To say I am nervous for this is a bit of an understatement.

I don't even know why, it's not like I haven't been on dates before. So, what the fuck is wrong with me?

Zeke's words from earlier put me at ease a little, but not as much as I would like.

I take a deep breath and open my door. I watch as Remy's eyes trail down my body and then back up, a smile forming on his face.

"Hi," I say almost breathlessly as I take him.

His eyes meet mine and they darken.

"Hi," he replies as he crosses his arms over his chest and leans on the door frame.

Holy fucking hell, if he keeps doing stuff like that, we won't be leaving my apartment.

"Eliza, if you keep looking at me like that, we won't be leaving this apartment," Remy says with a smirk on his beautiful face.

My eyes snap to his. It's as if he read my fucking mind.

I tell him, "I don't mind that."

He lets out a low moan and I pull my bottom lip in between my teeth.

"As much as I want to take you to your fucking bed right now," Remy says. "I also really want to take you on this date and do right by you."

I raise an eyebrow at him, and he hisses, "Goddamn woman."

A smile breaks over my face and he groans.

It takes everything in me to keep my eyes on his face.

"Alright big boy," I say as I pat him on the chest. "I'll somewhat put you out of your misery."

I lightly push his chest, so he'll move back, and he snatches my hand. He doesn't let go as I close and lock my door; he just twines our fingers together.

"Are you going to tell me what we're doing now?" I ask as we start down to the lobby.

"Nope," Remy replies popping the p. "But I can tell you that it's not a movie, because I don't think those are great for first dates."

"Agreed," I say. "You can't get to know someone in a darkened auditorium."

"And with my luck I'd end up choosing one that you've worked on."

I let out a laugh as I see the smile on Remy's face.

"That's okay," I reply. "Always gives me a chance to see it without worrying about the edit, and it's a good way to give credit to everyone that worked on it. Though you should know that I am one to sit through all the credits, even if there isn't a post credit scene."

"I wouldn't expect anything else," he hums and opens the passenger door of his truck for me.

As he closes the door and rounds the front to hop in on the driver's side I slip a piece of paper with my number on it into the cup holder. I hope he doesn't see it until later.

"I just hope you enjoy what I've got planned," he says with a hint of nerves in his voice.

I grab his hand and truthfully reassure him, "I'm sure I'll enjoy whatever it is."

"Don't be so sure," he says as he squeezes my hand.

I squeeze back and assure him, "I'm with you Remy, so I know I will."

The entire drive we make easy conversation with each other, and when there are silences, they are never awkward which is a little shocking.

When we pull into the arena, I'm so confused.

"Um do you have to pick something up?" I ask.

"Nope, just follow me," Remy replies and turns off his truck.

"Um okay."

He gets out and opens my door for me.

We walk into the arena, and it's so weird being in here when it's empty. I'm so used to it being bustling with people as they gear up to watch a hockey game.

"I feel like this would be a great place to film some kind of thriller movie," I say as Remy leads me to the tunnels. "Especially if most of the lights are turned off."

He lets out a laugh and replies, "I've never really thought about how creepy this place might be when empty."

I laugh at his response and say, "Well I am the creative here."

I can see his smile as we get to the players benches, and he pulls me in to sit down.

"Wow it all looks so different from this angle," I say as I look around. "I'm used to being near the penalty boxes."

Remy pulls out some skates and tells me sheepishly, "I wasn't sure what size you wear, so I just got multiple."

I reach up and cup one of his cheeks with my hand.

"You could've just asked what my shoe size is," I reply gently, and he ducks his head.

"I'm realizing that there's a lot that I could just ask you."

"Me too," I smile.

I grab the size 12s and work to take off my Chucks. Remy gets his skates on faster than I can get my shoes off and he kneels down to help me.

He's slipping off one of my shoes and starts to laugh.

"What?" I ask, not knowing what he is finding funny.

He lifts my foot and asks, "Are these aliens fucking surfing?"

A smile breaks over my face as I tease, "You have a problem with my socks Remington?"

He laughs again and says, "No not at all, I think they're awesome."

"Good," I reply through a laugh. "Because if you had a problem with my socks then we'd have a problem. All I have I are socks like this."

He slips my other foot out of my shoe and slides the skates on.

"I think it's very you, Eliza," he says. "And I'm still getting to know you."

Once he gets my skates tied, Remy stands up and holds his hands out. I grab onto them, and he pulls me up. I wobble for a second before steadying.

Slowly Remy leads me to the ice.

"I think that you should know I haven't skated in," I quickly do the mental math. "Eighteen years."

Remy stops and stares at me for a moment.

"I'm sorry," he says. "What?"

"I haven't skated in eighteen years," I reply.

"I heard you; I'm just trying to comprehend what you said."

He steps down onto the ice and moves his hands to my hips as I step down.

My feet almost come out from under me, but Remy is there to steady me. We stand there for a few minutes while I get my bearings.

"So how old were you then?" he asks curiously.

"Seven, I believe," I reply.

"So how old does that make you now?" he asks.

I don't tell him that he can do the math.

"Trying to get a girls age? Sneaky, sneaky," I tease. "I'm twenty-five."

"I'm almost thirty," he replies and slowly start skating backwards. "I'll be thirty in December."

"Good thing I've always had a thing for older guys," I say as I wink at him.

I think that affects him more than he wants to let on because he just about trips over his feet, and there's a slight blush to his cheeks.

"Jesus Christ woman," he hisses. "You really might be the death of me."

I squeeze his arms as I look down at my feet for a second.

"Now, now we wouldn't want that now would we?" I tease as we slowly start to move.

After a moment Remy asks, "What happened the last time you went skating?"

"Well, dad was taking me to see my best friend at the time at the IceForum, and that was the first time I'd been ice skating. After falling on my ass a few too many times, I spent the rest of the time holding on to my dad as we skated."

Remy lets out a sharp laugh, and I hit him on the chest.

"It's not funny Remington!" I exclaim.

He holds up his hand with pinched fingers as he replies, "It's a little funny."

"You're wounding my seven-year-old self."

"Sweetheart you did that all on your own," he says through a laugh.

I narrow my eyes at him as I try to ignore the feeling that washes over me after hearing him call me "sweetheart."

As we make a slow circle around the arena, I get more and more comfortable skating with Remy doing most of the work.

CHAPTER 19
REMINGTON

'm not kidding about Eliza being the death of me, though I do think that would be a fantastic way to go out.

Ever since she opened her door in that cropped hoodie, I've wanted to just say fuck it all and take her to bed. This is the first time I've seen her in anything besides a jersey in real life, and goddamn her body is a dream. Even if I haven't truly seen it yet.

Every small movement she makes, makes her hoodie ride up a little and shows a little bit of her skin. I have to work very hard not to throw her over my shoulder and run off somewhere to fuck her.

"I think you should know," Eliza starts. "That I usually hate first dates, simply because of all the small talk that you have to do, and with how awkward they often are."

We make our way through one lap, and I'm surprised how well Eliza is doing, even if I'm doing most of the work.

"Me too," I reply honestly. "It's just superficial stuff, and it doesn't actually let you get to know a person or if you want to go on another date."

Eliza nods.

We make another lap around.

Eliza asks when we are almost back at the benches, "Is it weird that I feel like I've known you for longer than I actually have?"

I shake my head and reply, "No, not at all, because if I'm being honest, I feel the same way."

She lets out a short laugh, and I swear her laugh is the most beautiful sound I've ever heard.

"Glad I'm not the only one that feels like they're going crazy," Eliza says. "I hate to admit it, but I think Zeke was right."

She shudders as if admitting that her brother is right about something physically pains her.

"What was he right about?" I ask as I step up into the benches.

"You likely feeling the same way as me."

We take to the benches and just sit there for a few minutes taking everything in. I can see the sweat running down Eliza's face, but she doesn't seem to mind.

"Come on," I say. "Let's get some food."

"Are we getting rink side service or are we getting out of these skates?" she jokes.

I tap my chin as if I'm thinking about the options she's presented.

"I think we can take them off," I reply as I swoop down and toss her over my shoulder.

She lets out a shriek.

"Remy! Let me down!" she exclaims.

"I don't think I will. I have a nice view of your ass from here."

I lightly slap her ass and leave my hand on the curve of it.

She shrieks again and says, "Oh yeah well I have a pretty good view of *your* ass."

I'm expecting her to slap my ass but instead she pinches me, causing me to clench my cheeks and jump.

I set her down as gently as I can only to find a huge grin on her face. I cup her cheek with my hand and smash my lips against hers. My other hand makes its way into her hair. I feel Eliza melt against me and her hands tease the hem of my shirt, barely touching my skin. This first kiss is far better than I could have ever imagined.

I growl into her mouth as my tongue meets hers and deepen the kiss even more. She lets out a moan and I move to lift her up.

Eliza's legs wrap around my waist as my hands rest under the curve of her ass to keep her up.

She pulls back, breaking the kiss and breathlessly asks, "I don't want our first time to be in a hockey rink. And if we keep going, we might end up there."

I place my forehead on hers and nod.

"I know," I reply.

We stay like that for a few more minutes before I slide her down my body to put her back on her feet. I know she's felt how hard I am when she lets in a sharp breath and her eyes darken slightly.

As quickly as we can we put our shoes back on, and start to head out of the arena.

"What if we just say fuck it to eating and just go back to my place?" Eliza asks looking at me through her eye lashes.

I roughly capture her mouth in mine and say between kisses, "I think that's a wonderful fucking idea."

CHAPTER 20
ELIZA

When we get back to my apartment Remy barely has enough time to close the door behind him before I grab the front of his shirt and pull him towards me. I smash my lips against his and when he opens his mouth to let me in, I gently bite his bottom lip.

He groans and pushes me up against the wall, and my hands go into his hair. Remy leaves my mouth and starts to trail down my neck. I pull on his hair as he sucks on my pulse point.

Remy's magnificent hands slip up under the hem of my hoodie and skim down my sides, before moving down to under the curve of my ass.

He pulls away for a second and asks, "Is your brother here?"

I let out a frustrated groan and reply, "If he is I'll kill him."

"I just don't need him to hear how loud I'm gonna make you scream."

With that he lifts me up and I wrap my legs around his waist, and I can feel that he's already hard. Though from what I could feel earlier, I think he's been hard since leaving the arena. Pulling his lips back to mine I thrust my hips against his.

"Keep doing that sweetheart, and you're going to make me come in my pants like a fucking teenager," Remy growls.

I do it again and reply, "Then take me to bed hot shot."

He kisses me hard, almost like I'm the oxygen that he needs right now. I waste no time in kissing him back just as hard and desperate.

Still wrapped around his waist, he starts to move away from my front door.

"Down the hall," I say, momentarily breaking our kiss. "To the right."

He captures my lips again and moves down the hall.

Remy tosses me onto my bed and takes a moment to look me over, before kicking off his shoes and moving to take my socks and shoes off.

"Take your shirt off," I demand.

"Little bossy aren't we?" he teases but grips the back of his shirt and pulls it over his head.

He tosses it to the side, and I move to sit up. I lick my lips as my eyes trail over his stomach muscles, and my eyes catch on the dark trail of hair that leads into his pants.

I reach forward and unbutton his pants, but Remy grabs my hands before I can do anything else.

"If you do that I won't last long," he growls.

"Not a problem with me," I reply.

His eyes darken and he says lowly, "Darlin' if anyone's coming first it's going to be you."

In one swift movement he pulls my hoodie over my head and tosses it next to his shirt. His hands immediately cup my breasts through my bra, and I can feel my nipples harden as he runs his thumbs over them.

"Goddamn Eliza. Your tits are amazing," Remy says pulling down the cups of my bra.

I shiver slightly as he rolls one of my nipples between his fingers.

"Are you a tits or ass guy?" I ask through a moan.

"When it comes to you," he replies. "Both. Now scoot back to the headboard."

I'm already soaking wet, but if he keeps using that voice with me I might just come from that alone.

Remy licks his lips as his eyes roam over me, "I can't wait to see what you look like completely naked."

I watch as he unzips his pants and pushes them down his hips. My eyes drop to the outline of his cock in his boxer briefs, and my mouth starts to water. I want to taste him so bad.

He pushes his underwear down, causing his dick to spring free and he gives himself two hard pumps before moving to pull off my pants.

I reach behind me and unclasp my bra, tossing to the side.

Steeping out of his pants, Remy crawls up my body and takes one of my nipples into his mouth. As he swirls his tongue over the tip and gently bites down. I let out a loud moan and lift my hips trying to find any kind of friction.

Remy's hands grip my hips and prevents me from moving.

"Do you like that, Eliza?" he asks. "I bet you'll be a writhing mess once I'm inside you."

I let out another moan as I try to lift my hips again.

"Well chop chop hockey boy," I say. "If you want to eat me out or make me come on your fingers, then it will have to wait for next time."

"I can see how wet you are from here, even through your underwear," he replies.

"Remy, please," I beg.

He quickly pulls my underwear off and reaches down to his pants, pulling out a condom. He quickly tears it open and rolls it on. He runs the head of his dick through my folds and taps my clit a couple of times before lining up with my entrance.

He stays there for a second and meets my eyes.

"Remington, if you don't stick your dick in me in the next three seconds, I swear to god," I say feeling the edge of an orgasm already.

He gives me a cocky grin and slowly starts to enter me, allowing me time to adjust to his size.

"Oh my god," I moan. "Holy fuck."

He takes one big thrust and seats himself to the hilt and says, "I'm no god baby, but I can make you see him."

I wrap my legs around his waist so he can get deeper.

Remy hasn't started moving yet, and I desperately need him to. Otherwise, I'm going to start moving myself, and I don't think Remy will like that very much right now. I know he wants to be in charge this first time, and I am completely okay with that.

I grab the back of his head, smashing his lips against mine and lift my hips anyway.

He moans into my mouth, and that seems to be all the encouragement he needs.

Remy pulls almost all the way out before slamming back into me. My eyes roll into the back of my head, and I moan.

My hands claw down Remy's back and one of his hands digs into my hip. I'm sure I'll have bruises there tomorrow, but I don't care. I'll wear his bruises like a badge of fucking honor. His other hand snakes down my body and moves between us as he circles my clit before flicking it.

My hips lift up to meet his touch.

"I'm about to—" I don't finish my sentence before I shudder as my release crashes through me. "Oh my god Remy!"

"Fucking hell," Remy groans. "You're so fucking tight."

It only takes him two more thrusts before I feel his dick twitch inside me before he's spilling into the condom.

Once he finishes, he falls on top of me and we stay like that for a moment, breathing heavy, before he finally pulls out. We both wince at the loss of contact. Remy quickly removes the condom and ties it off.

After another minute he gets up and asks, "Bathroom?"

I point towards the bathroom door, and he returns a few seconds later with a damp wash cloth and cleans me up.

When he returns, he sidles up next to me and pulls the covers over the both of us.

Remy pulls me closer and gently puts my head on his bicep. He lazily runs his fingers up and down my side.

"That was hands down the best sex I've ever had," I say sleepily.

"Me too," Remy replies and kisses my forehead.

"I need a shower," I say.

Remy nips my lips with his teeth and says, "We can shower in the morning."

I'm almost asleep and he whispers, "Sorry I didn't last long."

I reach up and cup his face, making sure he's looking at me and reply, "We have all the time in the world."

He hums.

My eyes slowly close and Remy sleepily whispers, "Goodnight my Eliza."

CHAPTER 21
REMINGTON

wake up the next morning with Eliza's naked body wrapped around mine. I think back to last night, and her curvy body sprawled out on her bed as I ponded into her. Everything about last night was perfect, and dare I say it was the best sex I've ever had. I know I agreed with Eliza when she had originally said that last night, but I really meant it and I mean it especially now in the light of day.

Glancing down at Eliza's sleeping form, I can tell that she is still dead asleep on my chest. One of my hands moves to her hair and I tangle my fingers in her messy curls. My other hand moves to her hip and just rests there.

I'm pretty sure that my phone is still in the pocket of my jeans, but I don't dare to bend down to try and get it. I'm going to let Eliza sleep.

I look down at her again, and a content smile takes over my face as she drools slightly on my chest. I don't mind because I'm happy and content in this moment.

I close my eyes for a second, and I must have dozed off because when I open my eyes again it's a lot lighter in Eliza's room. My eyes roam back to Eliza, and I find her blueish gray eyes staring up at me.

"Hi," I whisper not fully trusting my voice.

She buries her face in my chest and runs her hand up and down the center of my abs.

She looks back up and replies, "Hi."

"Have you been up long?" I ask, running my hand that had been on her hip up and down her side in a slow movement.

Eliza lifts her head slightly and looks around as if looking for a clock before dropping her head back down on my chest.

"I don't think so," she replies.

I hum and kiss the top of her head.

"Do you know what time it is?" I ask, hoping we have time to stay here before I have to go to morning skate.

"Too early," she says as she reaches behind her for her phone. "Nine."

Eliza shows me the time on her lock screen. I smile at the picture because there are two film strips on either side of a figure walking through sound stages. I'm curious as to what it's from, and what her home screen looks like, but I don't ask. I can ponder over it later or ask her after she's had time to wake up.

"I'll probably need to leave about 9:30 or so, so I can stop by my apartment and get ready for morning skate."

She lets out a small groan and holds me tighter.

"Morning skate, then I'm yours the rest of the day until I have to get ready for the game. How's that sound?" I ask feeling her sentiment.

"If it was up to me, we'd just stay here all day. But the hockey gods call," she replies as she dramatically flops onto her pillow. "Oh my god." Her hands fly to her face. "That makes me sound like a fucking stage ten clinger."

I let out a laugh. "Then I guess we're in the same boat."

Eliza shakes her head at me.

I lean over, gently pull her hands away from her face, and capture her mouth in mine.

"How bout I make it up to you by making breakfast?" I ask.

She moans and says, "Sounds wonderful."

I kiss her again before throwing the covers off and stooping down to grab my boxer briefs before heading into her bathroom. I smile to myself as I feel Eliza's gaze rake over my naked form.

I quickly pee and pull my underwear on. When I come out, I find Eliza sitting on her bed in my shirt.

"Stay like that for a second," I tell her and quickly move to grab my phone.

"Why?" she asks, raising an eyebrow at me.

I smirk and ask, "Am I not allowed to take a picture of a beautiful woman?"

She taps her chin and says, "That depends. Are you gonna drop to your knees and bark like you want it?"

"Woof," I reply.

She bites her bottom lip and smiles at me. I quickly take a picture and make it my lock screen wallpaper before saying, "You play a dangerous, dangerous game Eliza."

Her smile widens as she stands up, my shirt falling just about mid-thigh on her.

"I know," she replies, patting my bare chest before walking into her bathroom. "That's the fun of it."

My eyes trail down her long, toned legs and back up. I can't help that my eyes land on the curve of her ass my shirt doesn't cover, and I swear I'm already a goner.

I don't wait and head towards her kitchen. Now that I'm not preoccupied with make sure Eliza came, I make myself at home.

Looking around I can see Eliza in every corner, from the huge bookshelves lining one of the walls in the living room, to some of the movie posters hanging around her apartment and even the vinyls she has under her record player.

My eyes catch on a case full of pucks. Making my way over to her mantle to get a closer look, I catch sight of the puck I gave her. I smile knowing that she not only kept it, but also that she has it prominently displayed, apart from her other pucks.

Eliza comes up behind me and wraps her arms around my

waist as she buries her face in my back. My hands automatically go to hers.

"I'm surprised that you kept it," I say staring at the puck.

She tightens her arms before genuinely asking, "Why wouldn't I?'

I shrug, not really having an answer for her.

"Zeke says I can be a sap sometimes," she says. "Even though I'm not an overall optimistic person, most of the time."

I turn around in her arms to see a hint of possibly sadness in her eyes.

I grip her chin between my fingers, and tilt her head up before telling her, "There's nothing wrong with that. I think it's fucking great that you want to keep that memory forever."

A smile breaks across her lips, and I bring mine to hers. This kiss is slow and methodical, unlike last night where they were all hot and rough.

"You promised me food," she says breaking our kiss.

I smile and reply, "Is that all I'm good for? Feeding you?"

Eliza smiles back. "You'll learn Remy that I'm really an easy girl to please. The way to my heart is through my stomach."

I let out a sharp laugh

"Alright then," I say. "Let's get you some food. Wouldn't want to starve my girl."

CHAPTER 22
ELIZA

Remy decides to make us pancakes, and we chat while he cooks them.

"If you don't mind asking," Remy starts. "What is the picture you have as your lockscreen?"

I smile, because I love getting this question, and respond, "It's from *The Fabelmans.*"

Remy looks over his shoulder at me with a questioning look before asking, "What is *The Fabelmans?*"

My smile widens. "It's a fictionalized version of Steven Spielberg's life."

"Is it any good?" Remy asks. I'm pretty sure he isn't just asking to ask; I think he's genuinely curious.

I shrug and reply, "I think so. We can watch it sometime, if you'd like."

"I would love that," he says as he smiles over at me.

"It's actually like my dream to work with Steven Spielberg," I say, not knowing why I felt compelled to share that with Remy.

He looks over at me and replies, "Really? That would be amazing!"

I smile. "That's not something that I share with just anyone, just so you know."

"Well, I'm glad you trusted me with that information," Remy replies, and I can hear how genuine he is in his voice.

I watch as he flips a pancake, and I'm glad he can actually flip them because I sure as hell can't to save my life.

Just as he is plating our breakfast, I hear my front door unlock and open.

I let out a frustrated groan and Remy asks, "What?"

"My dickhead of a brother is here," I reply just as Zeke comes around the corner.

"Do I smell pancakes?" he asks not even realizing that Remy is standing in my kitchen, wearing nothing but his boxer briefs.

Zeke tries to steal part of my pancake, but I slap his hand away.

"Get your own man to make you breakfast," I practically growl and Remy chokes back a laugh.

Zeke stops seeing with his stomach for a minute and finally looks around. He takes in my appearance first, noting that I'm in a t shirt that is like two sizes too big, and my underwear. Then his eyes finally flick to Remy, who is leaning up against the island as he eats his pancake, enjoying the show.

"Are you even wearing pants?" Zeke asks, turning back to me.

I give Remy an annoyed look before replying, "I have on underwear, dickhead. And what the fuck are you doing here?"

Zeke shrugs and says, "Well I was coming over to talk to you about how your date went."

"It's like you're trying to walk in on us having sex," I reply. "And like if you're into watching people that's cool, great on you for knowing you're into voyeurism. But I'm your sister and I will have to draw a line."

Remy holds back a laugh.

"Ha ha," Zeke deadpans. "Very funny."

I give him a sarcastic smile as I shrug and reply, "I try."

Zeke turns to Remy and holds out his hand as he says, "Hey man. I'm Zeke. Dipshit's brother."

Remy takes his hand and replies, "Remy, but I guess you already knew that. Nice to finally meet you."

"Sorry about interrupting y'all's morning," Zeke says, genuinely seeming to mean it.

I kind of hate how Zeke can just turn on the charm when he needs or wants to.

I glance at the clock on the microwave and let out a small sigh.

"It's okay," I say, surprising both men. "Remy has to get to morning skate soon anyways."

Remy glances at the clock.

"Shit," he curses. "You're right."

"I'll take care of your dishes."

He nods and rushes towards my room. Zeke raises an eyebrow at me. In return I just narrow my eyes at him, daring him to say something. Luckily, he doesn't, at least for the moment.

Remy comes back to the kitchen fully dressed, with his hoodie, minus the shirt I'm wearing.

He comes up to me and kisses me on the top of my head before confirming, "I'll see you later, okay?"

I turn to kiss his cheek and reply, "You better."

He smiles and turns to Zeke. "Nice meeting you man."

Zeke nods at Remy and I watch as he walks toward the door.

It takes Zeke all of a minute before saying, "You really, really like him if you're already having sleep overs."

I roll my eyes and get up to clean up from breakfast.

"And would it kill you to put on some pants?" he asks as he jokingly covers his eyes.

"It's my apartment Z," I reply. "I can walk around like Winnie the Pooh if I fucking want."

"But my eyes Lizzie. My beautiful eyes."

"We have the same eyes," I say before throwing his own words back in his face. "And it's nothing you haven't seen before."

"So, what'd y'all end up doing on your date?" Zeke asks as he plays with a pen he found.

I finish cleaning up and reply, "He took me ice skating at the arena."

"But you hate ice skating."

I sigh. "No, I don't. I've just only done it once before and wasn't good at it."

"Yeah, because falling on your ass is considered great," he teases.

I flip him off and move towards my room to put on some pants.

"Did you at least have fun?" Zeke asks as he leans up against my door frame.

"It was amazing," I say as I pull on my Atlanta Flames flannel pants.

I can hear the smile in his voice as he replies, "Good, I'm glad."

"Come on," I say "We probably have an hour before Remy comes back.

Zeke follows me to the living room and points out, "I know you said that you really like this guy, but I didn't really believe you about how fast you thought things were going until I saw it with my own two eyes."

I sit down on my couch and Zeke sits next to me as I ask, "Are you calling me a liar?"

"Well, I ain't calling you a truther," he says quoting *Drake and Josh,* one of our childhood favorites.

I smile at him and get comfy to tell him how I'm practically halfway in love with Remington Miller. Though if I'm being honest, I'm like ninety percent sure Zeke already knows that without me having to tell him

CHAPTER 23
REMINGTON

When I run by my apartment Krypto is yelling at me the second I walk through the door. I know my cat is strict about when he gets fed, so I know that his bowl will basically be empty from where I fed him last night.

As I walk towards Krypto's bowl he weaves between my feet, yelling at me as he rubs up against my legs.

I pick him up and say, "I'm sorry buddy, I was with Eliza."

He instantly starts purring and nuzzling his head against me.

Quickly I scoop him a little bit of food and set him down before making my way to my room to change.

I'm ready to get morning skate over with so I can get back to hang out with Eliza.

It's crazy how much I already feel for her, and we've not known each other long. Like this morning after I snapped that picture of her, I made it my lock screen wallpaper. I'm not the kind of person to do that, especially after one date. That feels more like a three months into a relationship kind of thing, but I can see myself having a future with Eliza. And that's kind of scary to think I already know that, but I know she feels similar just from the conversations we had yesterday.

Maybe this is what they mean when they say "when you know you know."

When I get back into my truck, I feel a piece of paper in one of my cup holders as I'm setting my protein shake down. I pull it out to find half printed half cursive handwriting that reads Eliza and her phone number.

I smile.

I have no idea when she had the opportunity to do that last night, or if she had already written it before our date and slipped it into the cup holder. Either way I quickly snap a picture of it to reference later and tuck the piece of paper into the back of my phone case. I'll program her number into my phone after morning skate so I'm less tempted to use it right now.

I'm sitting in my stall after morning skate as I program Eliza's number into my phone and send her a text.

ME

So I guess this means that I've earned having you number?

This is Remy by the way

THE FUTURE MRS. MILLER

I was wondering how long it would take you to find and this and use it

How was morning skate? Assuming that it's over

ME

Wishing I was with you. Though Krypto might be mad if I don't spend time with him

THE FUTURE MRS. MILLER

I can always come to yours

If that's ok

I smile and quickly glance around to make sure that no one is looking to give me shit.

ME

Yeah, that's perfectly fine as long as you don't mind a cat

I know we had discussed Krypto before, but that didn't necessarily mean that Eliza actually liked cats.

THE FUTURE MRS. MILLER

Are you fucking kidding? I fucking love cats

That draws a bigger smile on my face, and that's when I hear, "Check it out cap."

I look up to find Jake elbowing Grant and pointing my way.

"Who are you texting there, Ratatouille?" Grant asks as him and Jake walk over to me, though I suspect they already know the answer to that question.

I give them both a hard stare and reply, "None of your business."

"I bet it's his girl," Jake says.

"Ratatouille doesn't have a girl," Misha shouts from across the locker room. At least I'm pretty sure it was Misha. I can't always tell if it's him yet.

"He's trying to," Jake shouts back with a smug smile on his face.

I flip him and Grant off and turn to finish getting out of my gear.

"He didn't even deny it," Grant says to Jake.

Jake replies, "I know. I can't believe it."

The way that they are talking makes it sound like I'm the team's fuck boy, but I'm not. Now don't get me wrong, I like sex as much as the next guy, but I would rather have someone that I can see a future with than meaningless hookups.

"Come on Ratatouille," Jake says, a bit quieter. "Cap and I have both met the girl, and we're happy for you."

"Yeah Remy," Grant adds. "If we cross a line just put us in our places."

I sigh and turn back to face them.

"It's just new and I'm a little freaked out by how much I already feel for Eliza," I quickly whisper. "I don't want to ruin it."

They both nod.

Grant slaps me on the shoulder and asks, "Have you told her this?"

I nod and reply, "Yeah and she feels the same way."

Jake says, "So you're both in this together?"

I let out a small laugh and reply, "Yeah, I guess so."

"Then everything will work out," Grant says.

I hope so.

They return to their own stalls to finish up.

My phone dings and I'm expecting it to be Eliza, but instead it's the group chat I have with Grant, Jake, and a couple of our other teammates.

PUCK HANDLERS UNLIMITED

CAP

See you boys tonight. Also we could potentially be adding a WAG in the future

SMITTY

And it's not cap

ME

MISHA THE RUSSIAN

ooh

BURNSIE

Want to share with the class Ratatouille?

ME

Fuck you all

I can hear them snickering as I pull my shirt on and sit down to tie my shoes, only to realize I didn't reply to Eliza.

ME

Sorry. Some of the guys distracted me.

THE FUTURE MRS. MILLER

No worries. Gotta answer when the hockey gods are calling

I let out a quiet laugh and send her my address as I start of out of the locker room.

ME

I'll be home in like 15. You can come over whenever

THE FUTURE MRS. MILLER

I'll be there in like 30. I have to get rid of the dickhead first

ME

😂. I guess I shouldn't be surprised he's still bugging you

THE FUTURE MRS. MILLER

He's currently trying to look over my shoulder as I type

Remind me to change my locks

Actually don't do that. I can't be deprived of my sibling time

I let out a laugh at the message Zeke sent. I can just imagine Zeke stealing Eliza's phone and then her doing everything she can get him to give it back to her.

ME

Hi Zeke.

THE FUTURE MRS. MILLER

Damn. I was hoping you wouldn't notice

Dickhead I tell ya. I think it's a miracle that I didn't swallow him in the womb

I'm about to pee my pants with how much I'm laughing.

ME

See you in a bit Liz

THE FUTURE MRS. MILLER

See you in a bit babe

Fuck. I can't believe I just did that

Double fuck. We've been on one date (technically two) and slept together once and now I'm panic rambling.

Getting into my truck I smile. It's endearing watching her panic text.

ME

It's ok. I'm surprised it wasn't me first

THE FUTURE MRS. MILLER

You don't hate me for dropping the "babe" when we don't yet have a label?

ME

I did technically call you my girl earlier and I could never hate you

THE FUTURE MRS. MILLER

Phew. Ok good. See you soon

I smile and start towards my apartment.

CHAPTER 24
ELIZA

Once I finally get Zeke to leave, I slip on some shoes and head towards Remy's building. Luckily there are a couple of guest parking spots that I am able to pull into.

When I walk into the building I'm greeted with Remy's doorman.

"How can I help you today?" the man asks.

"Um I'm here to see Remington Miller," I reply.

The man looks at something on his computer screen and asks, "Eliza Fox?"

"Yes," I reply.

"I'll let Mr. Miller know that you are on your way up," he says.

I smile and reply, "Thank you."

"Top floor dear."

I nod and head to the elevator. I feel so fucking underdressed. I'm now wishing that I had at least changed out of my flannel pants, but I'm comfy and didn't really think about it.

When the elevator opens up on the top floor, I'm greeted with a short hall leading to a single door.

As I get up to it I take a deep breath, and raise my fist to knock. Before I can get my fist on the door, it's swinging inward.

Remy looks me up and down and grins at me as he says, "Hi."

"Hi," I reply with a smile. "You gonna let me in, or make me stand out here?"

He quickly moves out of the doorway and says, "Right. Sorry. Welcome to my home."

I look around as I kick off my shoes and lock eyes with his cat.

Remy see what I'm looking at and warns, "Just a heads up, Krypto doesn't really like strangers, so he might run and hide."

"That's okay," I reply, knowing full well it will actually make me sad if Krypto runs.

Slowly I start walking towards Krypto. When I get close enough, I hold out my hand and squat down.

"It's okay buddy," I say. "I'm not going to hurt you."

Krypto looks at me for a moment before butting his head up against my hand. I scratch his head and move to pick him up. Krypto immediately starts purring as I hold him on his back in my arms.

"That's a good boy," I tell him as I rock side to side slightly.

"Holy shit!" Remy exclaims. "He's never like this."

I shrug and say, "I think cats are good judges of character."

"I'm a little upset that you're wearing pants," Remy tells me as he steps closer. "I enjoyed those long legs on display this morning."

"I couldn't leave without pants on," I reply and nuzzle Krypto. "And I had put them on to put Zeke at ease."

Remy leads me to his couch, and I have to put Krypto down to settle in on the couch next to Remy. It doesn't take long for Krypto to jump up on my lap.

"So, I've met your dad and brother," Remy says as he turns on the tv. "What about your mom?"

I knew it was coming, but I honestly didn't care. It has to come out at some point, and honestly, I'd rather it be sooner rather than later.

I shrug and reply, "I don't know where she is. She left when Z and I were about six months old."

I feel Remy tense next to me, and I turn to look at him as a pained expression takes over his face for a second.

He runs a hand over his face and says, "Shit. I'm sorry."

"It's fine, really," I assure him. "I've had many, many years to come to terms with it. And it's part of who I am. And you were bound to find out eventually, it's not something that I would keep from you."

I pick up Krypto so I can turn around to sit in Remy's lap.

I place my hands on his cheeks and say, "Hey seriously. It's okay. Okay?" I wait for him to nod his head. "My mom left, big fucking whoop. We're better off without her."

"I just don't understand people that can leave their kids like that," Remy grunts.

I give him a sad smile and reply, "Yeah me either."

I feel he's not telling me something—and it might not even be something for *him* to say—but I know he'll share it with me if he feels he can.

Remy leans into my touch and says, "Tell me something unrelated."

I think a second before telling him, "I originally wanted to be a Disney animator."

"Really?" he asks.

"Yeah," I reply.

"That's so fucking cool! What changed?"

"I found editing."

I can see that he's genuinely impressed. It's not something that I tell people. Only those closest to me know that little tidbit.

"Would you like to watch a movie or something?" Remy asks me after a minute.

Krypto jumps out of my lap, and I stretch out on the couch. Remy doesn't hesitate to follow me and wedges himself between me and the back of the couch.

"I'd love to watch a movie," I reply.

We decide to watch the animated *How to Train Your Dragon,* and settle in.

About halfway through the movie I can tell that Remy is very close to taking a nap as I card my fingers through his soft black hair.

"What's your middle name?" I ask, because I want to know absolutely everything about this man.

"Remington," he replies.

I smile and ask, "What's your first name then?"

"Nashville," he says into my chest. "Please don't laugh."

I let that sit with me for a moment before saying, "I'm not laughing. I think it actually suits you."

He tightens his arms around me as I think on it.

"I guess it makes sense with your sisters being Georgia and Arizona," I point out.

His hands find their way under the shirt of his that I'm still wearing and says, "Yeah well you can blame my mother, Virginia, for that."

I let out a laugh at that.

"Rem," I reply. "I'm serious about liking Nashville, but why do you go by Remington?"

"When I started playing hockey, I decided that my hockey name was going to be Remington. Also figured I'd get picked on less if I went by that rather than Nashville."

"So, like a stage name?" I ask.

Remy hums in response.

"I like Remington, but I think I might like Nashville better," I tell him, genuinely.

He lifts his head and props his chin on my chest.

"You can call me either Remy or Nash," he says. "I don't mind. Most of my family calls me Nash."

I smile at him.

"Nashville Remington Miller. Has a bit of a nice ring to it, don't you think?" I reply.

He smiles up at me.

"I've never shared that with anyone else."

I give him a meaningful look and lean down to kiss his forehead.

"Thank you," I say. "How did your mom come up with your name?"

"It's either where I was conceived or where my parents found out they were pregnant with me. I don't remember anymore."

"Is it the same for your sisters?"

He nods and says, "Yep."

"Fun."

He lets out a laugh.

"So, what's your middle name or first?" he asks me.

"Grace," I say.

"Eliza Grace Fox," he purrs, and I fucking shiver.

"Oh, you're going to be the death of me," I groan.

"That's my line, baby girl," he says.

"I think you might be my dream guy," I reply.

"Now I think *you're* going to be the death of *me*."

I smile at him.

I hear the credit music and look up to see the credits starting to roll.

I reach over for my phone and open the Letterboxd app to log the movie.

Remy looks at the app and asks, "What's that?"

"An app that allows you to log and review movies and see what other people are saying and watching."

"That's cool."

I look at the time and ask, "What time do you have to leave for the game?"

He glances up at the time on my phone and says, "Like four-ish."

I sigh. "I guess that means you need to get ready soon."

"Yep."

My eyes widen as I make the realization that hockey players wear suits.

"I get to see your fine ass in a suit," I practically exclaim.

"You like a man in a suit?" Remy asks through a laugh as he raises an eyebrow at me.

I let out a groan and reply, "A fine ass man in a well-tailored suit. Panty melting."

"You're making it really hard to get ready. We could just stay here."

"You know this guy that I like is playing tonight, and I'd really like to watch his game."

Remy pinches my side, making me squeal.

He stands up and quickly tosses me over his shoulder, taking me to his bedroom where he tosses me onto his bed.

Remy makes me sit there and watch as he gets dressed. All I want to do is run my hands over him, but I just watch like a good girl.

"Good girl," he says fully dressed, and kisses the top of my head.

"Are you going home before the game?" he asks.

I nod and say, "I'm not going to a hockey game in flannel pants."

He gives me a grin and says, "Good. Wear this."

He hands me a thin box and I open it. Inside is a jersey identical to the other one I have. But when I pull it out, I see a different name stitched at the top.

"Can't have my girl showing up to my game with another man's name on her back."

I shiver. I like seeing this side of Remy, and how it does things to me.

"What happens if I don't wear it?" I ask.

He tilts my face up and replies, "Then you'll find out what happens to bad girls."

With that he walks away, and I'm left to pick my jaw up off the floor. Not only from his words, but also the way his ass fills out his suit pants. That image of him walking away is going to stay with me forever.

A couple week later Athena calls me.

"Hey," I say answering my phone as I put my bookmark in the book I'm currently reading.

"Are you home?" she asks in response.

I reply, "Yeah."

She doesn't say anything else and hangs up on me. A few seconds later there's a knock on my door. This isn't unusual for us. Usually if we're near each other's apartments we'll call before showing up, just to make sure the other is home.

I open the door and let Athena in as I ask, "What if I hadn't been here?"

She levels a look at me and says, "Liz, when you aren't actively working on a job if you aren't here, you're either at the bookstore or at a hockey game if it's in season."

I sigh, knowing she's right.

"Shouldn't you be on set directing?" I ask.

Athena replies, "We have the day off to get over the past two days being night shoots."

"Ah the dreaded night shoots."

While I might be an editor and am not typically on set, I do still know the pains of doing night shoots. I've been on a couple of sets where it was mostly filmed at night and if we didn't have taillights at the twelve-hour mark, the crew had every right to leave, and it got pretty close that night.

We get settled in on my couch and she jumps right into why she's here.

"Alright first," she starts. "Are you going to Cam's premiere this weekend?"

My eyes widen and I reach for my phone. Pulling up the calendar I see that it is in fact in my calendar.

"Shit!" I exclaim. "I can't believe I forgot."

Athena playfully hits me. "No fucking way you forgot."

"I did. I don't know how, it's been in my calendar for ages," I reply.

"Girl, you edited the damn film," Athena says.

Which makes this that much more embarrassing, especially since Cam went to school with me and Athena, where we became really close friends. I'm pretty sure that Athena was the one that introduced us in school.

Athena picks up her phone and makes a call, putting it on speaker.

Cam picks up and says, "Yo, yo, yo."

"Okay get this," Athena says. "Liza forgot that the premiere was happening this weekend."

"To be fair," I explain. "I have had it on my calendar since it was announced."

"Eliza!" Cam fakes hurt. "How dare you!"

"I'm pretty sure that it's all the hockey dick that she's getting from her new boyfriend that is distracting her," Athena says.

I slap her on the arm and reply over Cam's squeal, "He's not my boyfriend."

"Yet," Athena gives me a knowing look. "Seriously Cam, you should see them."

"Oh my god!" Cam exclaims. "I can't believe I'm missing this in person. Texts can only do so much."

"Thena, you haven't even seen us," I point out.

"Yeah, yeah," she waves me off. "Semantics."

"As much as I would love to keep chatting, ladies," Cam says. "I do still have a lot to get done before the weekend. And Eliza, I better see you there."

"Don't worry," I reply. "I'll be there."

As Athena hangs up, I think I hear the lock on my door turning, and I let out a sigh. Because of course my fucking brother can't stay away for long, especially if he has a string of away games coming up.

"Hello ladies," he says as he saunters into my apartment, noticing me and Athena.

"Hi Zeke," Athena shyly replies.

I've had the suspicion that they've both had crushes on one another at different points in time, but I've never had any definitive confirmation.

"What are you ladies talking about?" he asks leaning over the back of my couch, turning on his playboy charm.

"You," I reply. "And your nasty ass."

Zeke gasps, throwing a hand over his heart and exclaims, "My ass is perfect. Thank you very much."

"What do you want?" I ask.

"Am I not allowed to just visit my sister?" he replies.

I narrow my eyes at him.

Athena lets out a giggle and says, "You guys have this argument all the time."

She's not wrong. I'm pretty sure that because Zeke and I shared a womb he thinks he has free reign to do what he wants when it comes to me. All I ask is that he knocks, is that so hard?

I glance at the clock.

"Shit!" I exclaim. "I'm late."

"What are you late for?" Zeke calls after me as I hurry to get my shoes on and pull on a hoodie.

"A meeting with Brian and the rest of the post team," I reply. "If y'all leave before I get back, please lock up." I start out the door but turn back. "And no fucking in my bed."

I pull into a parking spot and quickly kill the engine. I'm not usually like this. First, I forgot about Cam's premiere, and then I almost forget about this little meeting.

I don't even really need to be here; I just know Brian mostly wants me here as support. I also think it's for the heads on the post team to get a more acquainted with one another, even if we are already familiar with each other. I don't really get it either.

About halfway through the meeting Remy texts me, and I can feel the smile forming on my face.

NASHVILLE <3

I miss you. When can I see you again?

ME

Do you want to see me or my pussy?

I can imagine the sound he makes when he reads my text, and it makes me feel good knowing how much I affect him.

NASHVILLE <3

I wouldn't mind seeing both

ME

Be a good boy and don't touch yourself and we'll see what your prize is

NASHVILLE <3

Tease

ME

Oh I do want to ask you something when we see each other again

NASHVILLE <3

Do I get to know now?

ME

Nope

I've been thinking about this for the last couple of days, I just haven't really known how to ask. And this isn't the kind of thing you go around asking just anybody. Same with how you don't ask just anyone to recreate the iconic Spiderman kiss with you.

ME

I'll be in LA for a premiere this weekend

NASHVILLE <3

I'll be home tomorrow and then I'm yours for three days.

ME

I can't wait for you to bury your dick inside of me

I have no idea if he's alone or not, but I like playing this game with him. I bet he can't keep a straight face from reading my messages, but I read smut for fun and know how to keep my poker face on.

NASHVILLE <3

Fucking hell Liza. I'm with the guys

ME

Brian asks me a question, breaking my bubble, "So Eliza, are you working on any new projects?"

"Um, technically," I reply. "But it's technically still in prepro."

"Cool, cool," he says as we exit the room.

"Well, it was nice seeing you again, Brian," I say as I head for the exit.

"Yeah, you too," I hear him say.

I don't dwell on the conversation and get in my Jeep to leave.

CHAPTER 26
REMINGTON

'm so fucking ready to get home so I can see Eliza and be able to sleep with her. I can only do so much with my hand, and it really doesn't compare. Though I guess I don't really have that option at the moment.

I'm also curious as to what she wants to ask me, because I have no clue what it could be. There's just so many things she could want to ask, and I can't exactly gauge her tone from a text.

We've only known each other about three weeks, but it feels like we've known each other longer. I've never felt this way about anyone before. Eliza fits so perfectly in my life, it's almost hard to imagine that there was a time before her.

I quickly stop by my apartment to drop off my stuff and take care of Krypto before heading off to Eliza's.

I know Krypto isn't too happy about this, but as long as he has food and water, he'll be fine. It's times like this that I'm so fucking grateful that I spent the money on an automatic litter box for him.

When I first found him, I had been very skeptical about bringing him home because of my crazy schedule. But he's honestly one of the best decisions that I've made, and I couldn't be happier that I decided to keep him after the cat distribution system put Krypto in my life.

I get to Eliza's apartment in record time, and in no time, I'm knocking on her door. She opens the door and locks eyes with me, and I watch the smile that takes over her beautiful face.

I take a step forward, grab her face with my hands, and smash my lips against hers.

She melts into me and immediately opens her mouth to let me in.

I kick of my shoes and start walking her backwards. Eliza's back hits the couch, and I pick her up and walk around.

I lay Eliza down on her back and climb on top, not breaking our kiss.

"Were you a good boy?" she asks.

"Baby I haven't touched myself in two days. So, I'm probably not going to last long," I tell her.

She smiles and says, "Good boy. Now make me come until I can't see straight."

"Holy fuck," I breath out.

I never thought that I was one to have a praise kink, but apparently Eliza brings out sides of me that I never knew existed. I also didn't really know that I would like dirty talk directed at me until Eliza.

I reach behind my head and grab the collar of my shirt, tugging it over my head. I toss it aside and watch Eliza's' eyes trail down my abdomen before putting her hands on my pecs. I shiver at her touch.

Slipping my hands under the hem of her shirt I slowly drag it up her body, until she's on her back in just her bra.

Pulling one of the cups down, I immediately put my mouth on her nipple, rolling it between my teeth and tongue.

Eliza arches her back and lets out a moan. And fuck if I don't almost come right then.

"Eliza if you don't behave, I'm going to come in my pants," I say.

She just moans in response as she trails her fingers down the ridges of my abs and starts to unbutton my pants.

I grab her hands and hold them above her head in one of my hands.

"You come first," I growl.

"You're no fun," she writhes as she pouts.

Instantly I capture her mouth in mine, and with my free hand I unhook her bra, tossing it to the ground.

She lifts her hips trying to find some friction. I place my free hand on her hip, making her put them back down.

"Are you wet for me baby?" I ask and she nods her head.

I yank down her shorts and say, "Look at you Liza. You're fucking soaked."

Through her underwear I tease her clit, and she moans. I can feel my dick straining against the zipper of my pants, and it's fucking painful, but she will come first.

Moving Eliza's underwear to the side I run my finger through the slickness of her folds. She lifts her hips again and groans when I remove my finger.

"Needy little thing," I tease. "Aren't you? What's the magic word Eliza?"

"Please," she begs.

I don't hesitate to plunge a finger into her and am greeted with a sinful moan. I lean down and place my tongue on her clit, and Eliza lifts her hips to my face.

I let go of her hands and use my free hand to pull her closer.

I insert another finger, causing Eliza to wrap her legs around my head.

"Fuck!" she exclaims. "Remy!"

I smile against her and pump my fingers into her.

Her legs tighten and she screams, "Oh my god!"

"Not God sweetheart," I reply. "Only me."

"Bastard," she moans, lifting her hips to meet my fingers.

I thrust my hips into the couch as I swirl her clit with my tongue.

"Oh god. Nash! I'm gonna—"

Eliza doesn't finish her sentence as I feel her tighten on my fingers, and her legs tighten around my head before she goes limp. I thrust into the couch a couple more times without thinking.

I feel the dampness in my pants before I really register it.

Eliza looks down and asks, "Did you—?"

I let out a sharp laugh and lick her arousal off my fingers.

"Yeah," I reply gruffly. "Are you proud of yourself?"

The smile she beams at me paired with the look in her eyes would definitely make me come in my pants if I hadn't already.

Eliza teases my happy trail before she answers, "Oh I'm so fucking proud of myself."

I let out a groan and climb up her body.

"That mouth of yours is going to get you in trouble," I say.

She quirks an eyebrow and replies, "You going to spank me for being a bad girl?"

I bury my face in the crook of her neck and reply, "Fucking hell Eliza."

She runs a hand through my hair as the other runs up and down my back.

"I missed you," she practically whispers.

I kiss her jaw and reply, "I missed you too, baby."

Eliza wraps her arms around my neck and holds me. I wrap my arms around her waist and just listen to her heartbeat.

I love every moment with Eliza, especially the small ones like this.

CHAPTER 27
ELIZA

made Remy come in his pants. I made Remy fucking *come* in his pants. Man talk about an ego boost. I didn't know could feel this way.

"What was it that you wanted to ask me?" Remy asks me from his spot on the couch as I come back from the bathroom sometime later.

"Um," I reply hesitantly. "It's completely fine if you say no. It won't hurt my feelings."

"I won't say no," he says as I step between his legs.

"Don't say that because you genuinely might."

He pulls me closer and assures me, "Baby, whether you realize it or not, I can't easily say no to you."

I squint my eyes and huff, "Okay, but let it be known that I did warn you."

He gives me a panty melting smile and says, "Hit me with your question baby."

I reach around him and grab my phone to quickly pull up my reference.

"Would you be willing to recreate this for me?" I ask as I show him the iconic picture of Johnny Depp wearing a crop top in *Nightmare on Elm Street*.

Remy stares as it for a moment then looks back up at me with a smile slowly spreading across his face as he says, "You're so fucking hot when you think that I won't do something for you."

I smile back at him and reply, "And you're so fucking hot for not having a fragile sense of masculinity."

He kneads my hip and asks, "So how many guys have you gotten to do this?"

I pretend like I'm thinking before answering, "You're the only one I want to paint you like one of my French girls."

He lets out a laugh and throws me over his shoulder as he stands up.

"You know I'm beginning to think you like having me in this position," I tease.

Remy lightly smacks my ass and replies, "It gives me a really nice view."

"Well, I've got an amazing view as well," I say as I look at his back muscles and trail my gaze down to his amazing ass, and how it fills out his shorts.

He slides me off his shoulder and tells me, "Alright Eliza, do your worst."

I pat his cheek and reply, "Go put your jeans back on and I'll get everything else.

"But Johnny was in sweats," Remy points out.

"Yes, but I want you in jeans, Nashville," I say. "Low on your hips. I wanna see that seductive v."

A shiver runs through him when I use his first name. I wasn't joking when I said that I like his name a few weeks ago, and I think he likes when I call him Nashville. I've been testing it out these past few weeks, and seeing if his first name rolls off my tongue well.

He presses a kiss to my head and hurries to retrieve his jeans from my drier.

I don't have a lot of crop tops, and I honestly have half a mind to just use an old t shirt and cut it for him. I decide against that as I find one that is football jersey material and deem that it will work. Though I don't know how well it will work since Remy is obviously larger than me.

Remy comes up behind me and I lift the shirt up for him to see and say, "It'd be better if it was a hockey jersey."

He pulls me against his chest and reaches out for it as he replies, "We can make that happen."

I tilt my head back to look at him. "I know you can, but I want to be able to see your arms."

"Do you have a thing for my arms?" he asks as he flexes.

"Free arm porn," I reply as I squeeze his bicep.

He laughs and takes the shirt from me. I watch unashamedly as Remy pulls it on and it lands just past his rib cage.

I bite my bottom lip and hold back a moan. Remy smirks at me and I can see him purposefully flex his ab muscles.

I let out a groan and his smile widens.

"Focus Eliza," Remy teases "You can ride me later, but right now I'm pretending to be Johnny Depp."

A shudder rolls through me.

"Fine," I say.

I walk past him and run a finger over his stomach, causing *him* to shudder. I smile to myself because two can play that game.

"Question," he asks after a minute. "How are we going to use a landline?"

I look at him and say, "Remy, I'm a filmmaker."

I know that only confuses him more, but I just open my hall closet instead of further elaborating. I grab one of the tubs stashed in there and start digging through it.

"Aha!" I exclaim victoriously.

Remy looks over my shoulder and says, "Liza it looks like the red Batman phone."

He's of course referencing the 1966 *Batman* starring Adam West. The one with the red phone that Commissioner Gordon primarily uses to get in touch with Batman.

"I know," I reply. "Like I said I'm a filmmaker."

"Eliza is this real or a prop?" he asks as if he doesn't want to touch it if it's real.

"A replica of a prop," I reply. "I have a bunch of stuff from short films I've helped make. Also, I told you my dad has a buddy that likes making movies props."

That seems to put him at ease. I don't blame him. If I thought that it might be real, I wouldn't want to touch it either, because something like that belongs in a museum.

I take the phone over to one of my bookshelves and direct Remy to stand next to it, with the sunlight hitting the left side of his face.

He picks up the handset and places the receiver on his ear.

Remy doesn't need me to tell him to rest his butt on the windowsill or to use his free hand to prop himself up, he does that all on his own. He crosses one foot over the other, and I just stare at him, because damn, that is everything. Not even that he looks so good like this, but that he is willing to indulge me in one of my fantasies.

I love you.

I don't voice that thought as I pull up the camera on my phone and get the framing right.

I snap a few pictures as he looks me up and down, and a smile takes over his face. As much as I love the candid photos I take of Remy, something about this one just does me in.

"Okay," I say after looking through the pictures, and choosing my favorite one.

I quickly set it as my lockscreen wallpaper without thinking then move to show Remy.

He wraps his arms around my shoulders and pulls me close. I let him flip through the pictures at his own speed.

"I like this one," he says.

"Me too," I reply. "It's my favorite."

"Will you send them to me baby?" he asks.

I nod and select the photos to send to him.

Remy kisses my shoulder and says, "All of them are really good. Next time you'll be the one in front of the camera."

"Sounds risqué," I tease.

Remy squeezes me.

His phone pings from my message and he moves to get it. I watch as he stands there for a moment as he types something out on his phone before closing it.

My phone dings and I think it's a text from him before seeing an Instagram notification from him tagging me in a post instead.

"What?" I asks as I open it.

Instagram loads into the post he just posted. It's one of the more neutral photos I took. I see the caption: my girlfriend thinks I rock this better than Johnny Depp.

My jaw drops.

"Since when am I your girlfriend?" I ask liking the picture and looking up at him.

Remy steps closer and says, "Since now if you want that."

"Don't fucking joke, Nash," I reply. "Of course I want to be your fucking girlfriend."

He wraps his arms around my waist and replies, "Good. Otherwise, this would've been so fucking awkward."

I let out a laugh and reach up to kiss him, and he kisses me back.

CHAPTER 28
REMINGTON

We're sitting on the couch watching a movie when my phone starts to ring. I pick it up and internally groan at seeing my mom's name on the caller ID. Don't get me wrong I love talking to my mom, but I have a feeling that she saw my post about Eliza and is calling to talk about that.

Since Georgia and Arizona found out that there might be something between me and Eliza, I've had a few conversations with my mom, but nothing extensive where she could interrogate me.

Eliza pauses the tv as I answer my phone and put it on speaker. I don't care if Eliza hears this; I have nothing to hide from her.

"Hi Mom," I answer.

My mom chides, "Nashville Remington. I thought I raised you better than this!"

I watch as Eliza bites her lower lip trying to hold back a smile as I reply, "And what would you be referring to this time, dear mother?"

Mom huffs and says, "You're supposed to tell your family that you have a girlfriend before announcing it to the world."

"I wasn't aware that I did."

Eliza tries to hold back her smile, but she quickly loses that battle. I love seeing the way it lights up her face.

"First, I had to find out from your sisters that you were talking to someone, and then I have to find out from Instagram that you have a girlfriend. I raised you better than this Nashville Remington," Mom says. "I know that you're a big hockey star now, but that doesn't mean that you can forget about your mother."

Eliza drops her head into her hand and looks up at me lovingly. We haven't said the big L word yet, but I already know that I fucking love her.

"Well Gigi and Ari should have never known that I was talking to anyone in the first place," I tell my mom. "They are just way too nosy for their own good."

Mom sighs and replies, "If not for them I probably wouldn't have known that you were seeing anyone."

"I would have told you when I was ready."

"Would you really have, Nashville?"

"Yes mother. Like I told G and Ari when they found out, I wasn't sure if there was actually anything between me and Eliza," I sigh. "I would have preferred to make sure that our relationship was a sure thing before telling y'all, but that's not how it happened."

Eliza gently places her hand on my bicep and rubs back and forth with her thumb. I place my hand over hers and give it a squeeze.

"Are you happy?" My mom asks.

I smile and reply genuinely, "Yeah. I am. She makes me so fucking happy."

"Good. I'm glad," Mom says. "Alright Nash, I have to go but I love you baby. And I expect to hear more about Eliza later."

"Alright. Love you, mom."

With that she hangs up and I turn to look at Eliza.

"I'm sorry about that," I say.

She smiles and replies, "It's okay. It's nice to know that your mom cares about you."

"Are you sure?" I ask, uncertain.

"Of course, Nash," she replies as she climbs into my lap. "I love that you love your mom and respect her, and I would never fault you for having a caring mom just because I don't."

I love you, I think.

I rest my hands on her hips and rest my forehead against hers.

"You are fucking magnificent," I say. "You know that?"

Eliza smiles and tangles her fingers in my hair.

"Am I now?" she teases.

I smile back and say, "Your dad did a fantastic job raising both you and Zeke."

I see a question starting to form on her face and decide just to tell her.

"Georgia is a single mom," I tell Eliza, and her eyes widen slightly in surprise. "Max's dad left her not long after she found out she was pregnant. And I know that's not really for me to tell you, but I feel that it's something that you should know."

Eliza's hands move from my hair to cup my cheeks.

"That's not Max's dad," Eliza replies. "That's his sperm donor. Just like the woman who birthed me and Zeke is our birth giver, not our mom. They have no claim to the name mom or dad."

I let that sit with me for a minute. Eliza's right, if I'm being honest.

"Does it suck that I grew up not knowing a mother's love?" Eliza asks. "Yeah, it fucking sucks balls, Nash, but my dad more than made up for it. And I bet Georgia does the same for Max."

I give her a sad smile. I can't believe I'm lucky enough to call this woman mine.

"I'm sorry for bringing up the mom thing," I tell her honestly.

"Nash, look at me," she says, and I do. "Never be sorry for

conversations that are bound to happen. Of course, you'd likely feel a little guilty about having a loving mom the first time after I told you about my birth giver. It's only natural, babe."

"I'm a little envious of how understanding you are about this," I reply.

Eliza lets out a small laugh and says, "Yeah well, I've had my whole life to comes to terms with it. And I've never understood why someone should feel bad about having a loving parent where someone else doesn't. It makes no fucking sense."

Now it's my turn to let out a small laugh. "Yeah, well the human brain makes no fucking sense."

"Try thinking about time travel."

We both start to laugh.

I'm glad that we can have these kinds of serious conversations without getting our feelings butthurt. It also helps that Eliza isn't one to dwell on how a serious conversation might affect her. She talks about it but doesn't let it bother her too much, and I think part of that has to do with her having to learn to be okay with her up brining.

If I'm being honest, it just makes me love her that much more.

"All right," she says when she finally composes herself. "Can we get back to the movie? I actually want to know what happens."

I kiss her temple and reply, "Whatever the lady wants."

She shakes her head as she climbs off my lap and curls up next to me as she turns the movie back on.

CHAPTER 29
REMINGTON

'm getting ready to head to the arena for our game tonight, and I am a mess. This will be the first home game I'm playing in that Eliza won't be at. In the short amount of time, we've been together she's so easily become part of my routine.

I'm pulling up my pants when Georgia calls me.

"What's up Gigi?" I ask as I put my phone on speaker.

"Since Thanksgiving is coming up in the next week or so," she starts. "The family wants to come to the game the day before."

"Okay," I reply as I sit down to pull my socks on. "That's nothing new."

Georgia sighs and asks, "Will you be able to watch Max the night before?"

"You know I love Max, but can't mom or Ari watch him?"

"No because Ari is picking Mom and Dad up to bring them here and I trust you."

My family lives close to Charleston, South Carolina, which is close enough to Atlanta that it's nice. It's also far enough away to be a bit of a nuisance.

"Wait why do you need someone to watch Max?" I ask as I put some food in Krypto's bowl.

"Because I need some me time, Nash," Georgia replies. "And I'm looking to possibly go on a date."

Like I told Eliza, Georgia's ex, Max's father, left them shortly after she found out she was pregnant. Ever since she's been raising Max on her own. Max will be turning three in March, and I know being a single parent wears down on her.

I let that sit with me for a moment as I think about Eliza's dad, and how he had to raise Eliza and Zeke by himself. I make a mental note to get Eliza and Georgia to talk about that.

"Yeah, I'll watch Maxie," I say not needing to ask any more questions.

"Thank you, Nash!" Georgia sighs, relieved. "You big brother are a life saver."

"Yeah, well I have a game to get to," I say.

"I'll give you more details when I get them," she replies.

We say our goodbyes and hang up

As I'm walking to my truck I text Eliza.

ME

What are you doing for Thanksgiving?

THE FUTURE MRS. MILLER

Other than going to Z's game nothing on the actual day. But Z, dad, and I will go out to eat that Friday. Why?

ME

Trying to make plans with my girlfriend

THE FUTURE MRS. MILLER

She sounds hot

ME

Trust me baby, she's a smoke show

When I get to the arena I go through my routine, trying not to think about Eliza not being here. I already know that this is going to be tough, there's no denying that.

When I step out of the tunnel and onto the ice, my eyes immediately drift to where Eliza normally sits. I don't find her, instead, I just find her dad. At first, I don't notice him subtly motioning me over, but when I catch on, I skate that way.

Jeremiah makes his way down to the glass and tosses something over when I reach him.

I catch it and notice it's a small baggie with a note and a bunch of Hershey Kisses.

I pull off my glove and get the note out to read.

When I open it I smile at Eliza's semi messy handwriting that is a mixture of print and cursive, and read.

> Since I can't be there tonight to kiss you good luck, Nash, I figured some Hershey Kisses would have to do. I don' think my dad would kiss you for me, and you don't want Zeke kissing you.
>   <3 Eliza

I let out a laugh and look up at Jeremiah.

Thank you, I mouth to him.

He nods and turns to go back to his seat.

I skate back to our bench and get the attention of our equipment manager.

"Hey Zack," I say. "Can you put this in my locker?"

I hand him the bag with the note tucked back in it.

He takes it and replies, "Yeah, no problem, man."

"Thanks."

Even though Eliza isn't here, she still managed to make her presence known. Knowing she'd been thinking about me and my routine makes it easier to play. I'm learning that she's right about the fans being just as—if not more—superstitious as us players.

By the end of the game, we're up three to one and it feels good to have the win, even without my girl here.

When I get back to my stall, I see the Kisses and grab my phone to text Eliza only to find a couple of messages from her already.

THE FUTURE MRS. MILLER

You probably won't see this until after the game but don't forget I'm a hockey fan, I'm also superstitious when it comes to my team

The second message is a video. I click it open having no clue what I will find.

It starts on a screen recording of her watching the game, then she exits that app and goes to the camera app. When she tilts her phone, I see that she's on the red carpet. I read the words written under the whole video that says, "is this a good place to be watching hockey?"

I laugh at her video.

I've learned that while Eliza might professionally work in the film industry as an editor, she still like making silly little videos like this, and can make them in no time.

ME

There's never a bad place to watch hockey

I don't expect her to reply right away, but she does.

THE FUTURE MRS. MILLER

True

ME

Aren't you walking the red carpet or something?

She sends me a selfie of her eating popcorn.

THE FUTURE MRS. MILLER

Waiting on the fancy pants people to get here
so we can get this show on the road

ME

Do you go to film premieres often?

THE FUTURE MRS. MILLER

Only when I edit one of my friends films. Or if
I'm invited.

Jake walks up to me as I'm pulling off the rest of my gear and asks, "Are you gonna come out with us tonight?"

"Why not," I reply. "I guess I can celebrate with my team for once."

Jake pumps a fist in the air and exclaims, "Yes! That's what I'm talking about. Bring Eliza if you want."

"Can't," I reply. "She's in LA for a film premiere."

I show him the video and he asks, "Do you think she's worked with lots of big name actors?"

I shrug and say, "I don't know, but I know that she doesn't usually get to work with the actors."

Jake shrugs and replies, "It's still fucking cool what she does."

"Yeah, it is."

ME

Going out with the boys tonight to celebrate

THE FUTURE MRS. MILLER

Have fun. Movie is starting soon, so I'll talk to
you later

I start to type out "I love you" but quickly delete it. I know our whole relationships has moved fast, but I fear that might scare Eliza off.

I rake a hand through my hair and take a deep breath. I know the both of us are on the same page about seeing a future with one another, but I don't know if she's ready to hear that I love her. I don't want to risk running her off because I know for a fact that she would take my heart with her. And I can't say that I would recover from that.

ME

Have fun

When I get home from Los Angeles all I want to do is fall onto my bed, but I have plans on surprising Remy at his game tonight.

"Hurry up Liz!" my dad calls from my living room as I drop my stuff off and grab my jersey. "We can't miss puck drop!"

"Dad," I reply pulling the jersey over my head and walking back towards him. "The doors don't open for another forty minutes. We'll be fine."

"Still," he says. "I don't want to risk missing puck drop."

I roll my eyes. I'm thankful that he was willing to pick me up from the airport, but he's so worried about getting to the game on time even though he knows we will. I honestly don't understand the way he thinks sometimes, but also, we're so alike it's kind of scary.

You would think my dad and I were the hockey players with how superstitious we've become as hockey fans. Seriously we weren't always like this, but a couple of years ago when the Flames were in the semifinals for the Stanley cup, we found ourselves doing the same thing for the games if we thought they worked in the previous one.

I'm closing the passenger door when my dad asks, "Does Miller know you're going to be there tonight?"

"No," I reply buckling my seatbelt. "I wanted to surprise him."

"You should invite him to our Thanksgiving dinner," dad says.

"Why?" I ask, even though I have already thought about it.

Dad sighs and replies, "So we can meet him."

"Dad, y'all have already met Remy."

"I know, but this is in an official sense, as your boyfriend."

"Yeah alright. I'll ask him about it."

Dad nods and heads towards the arena.

After grabbing some food, we head to our seats. The team is already out for warmups, and my eyes trail over the players until I see the number 26.

Remy is facing away from our seats, but one of his teammates locks eyes with me. He nudges Remy and points in my direction. He turns around, eyes searching. When they lock on mine, I can see the smile that takes over his face before he skates over.

Hi, he mouths to me.

I can feel the smile take over my face as I mouth back, *Hi.*

He opens his mouth to say something before holding up a finger and skating off. I watch as he talks to one of the crew members before being handed something and skating back over to me.

As he gets closer, I see that he's writing on a white board. I can feel a smile starting to tug at my lips seeing him like this.

When he gets back to me, he holds it up and I read:

How are you here?

I pull out my phone and type up my response in my notes app.

`A thing called a plane.`

Remy gives me a look and writes,

Ha ha very funny.

I smile at him.
Talk more after the game?
He reads it and nods before writing one more thing.

See you then baby.

I'm sitting back down in my seat to eat as I say to my dad, "If I find out you told Z about this, I will disown you."

My dad lets out a sharp laugh before replying, "I don't have to tell him. He saw with his own two eyes."

I whip my head around to find Zeke jogging down the stairs with a shit eating grin on his face.

"What the fuck is he doing here?" I ask my dad.

"I invited him," dad replies, the meddler that he is.

I whip my head back to Zeke and ask, "What the fuck are you doing here? You don't watch hockey."

"What? I can't just want to spend time with my family?" Zeke asks, feigning innocence.

"I fucking hate you both," I say.

"Dad did you see her having a romcom moment with her boyfriend?" Zeke asks sitting next to me.

Dad pops a Reese's in his mouth and replies, "I sure did Z."

"I'm gonna kill the both of you," I grumble. Leaning over Zeke I ask, "You couldn't have had another girl? Instead, I'm stuck with this bastard." I look at Zeke. "I should've eaten you in the womb when I had the chance."

"I'm older," Zeke responds. "So that technically means that you were the oopsie."

I let out a gasp and ram my elbow into his ribs as dad says, "Uncalled for Ezekial. Now both of you behave."

I give Zeke a seething look and turn my attention back to the ice as the team finishes with their warmups.

As the game wears on, my eyes keep drifting towards Remy. I can't help when my eyes leave the puck to find him, but each time I do I feel a small smile on my face that I pray Zeke doesn't see.

This game is electric. The Washington Jets aren't playing clean, which means that the Flames aren't either. One thing about my team is that they aren't going to lay down and just take the shit the other team gives them, no, the Atlanta Flames will go down swinging.

The problem with that is the fucking refs are calling more penalties on us rather than the Jets. I hate when refs clearly have a favorite team, and you can always tell with how they call things. On the bright side though I get to see a lot of Remy, because he is no stranger to the sin bin. None of our guys are though, well maybe except the goalies but they're special.

I fear dad and I will lose our voices by the time the game is over because we keep screaming. Zeke too, but he only understands so much when it comes to hockey. At least he's not trying to root for the Jets. One thing about Zeke is that, just like me, he's a die-hard Georgia sports fan. You won't ever catch us wearing Tennessee orange or something like that for anyone, it's the Georgia Bulldogs or nothing.

"Come on ref!" I yell. "Open your fucking eyes and call the damn penalty!"

I swear I see Remy trying to hold back a smile a few of the times that he's in the box and I yell at the stupid refs. Like now I'm pretty sure he's trying his damndest not to get his head out of the game.

I can't wait until the game is over and I can talk to him.

CHAPTER 31
REMINGTON

When I had gotten to the arena for tonight's game the last thing I had expected to see was Eliza's beautiful face in the stands. But holy fucking shit when Jake pointed out someone in the crowd only to turn around to find Eliza, I was fucking floored.

I hadn't expected to see her until later or even until tomorrow, but I'm so fucking glad that she's here.

"Ratatouille," Grant says as he skates over to me. "I'm surprised you aren't raging about the guy talking to your girl right now."

I look over to where Eliza is again and see her ribbing Zeke.

"That's just her brother," I reply.

Axel Burns, one of our defensemen, looks over to where Eliza is and says, "Holy fuck. That's Zeke Fox."

"Yeah," I reply unfazed. "Eliza's brother."

I watch his eyes bug out of his head as what I said connects in his head.

"Holy fuck, Ratatouille!" he exclaims. "You've been holding out on us."

"Who's been holding out on us?" Misha Petrov, our other first line defenseman asks.

Jake has a smug smile on his face as he replies, "Ratatouille's girlfriend's brother is Zeke Fox."

"Shit, Rem," Petrov says. "You lucky bastard."

These are professional hockey players in the NHL freaking out over a football player. Granted he is one of the best tight ends in the country but still.

"Have you met him?" Burns asks.

I nod and reply, "Yeah, briefly."

"You are so lucky, you fucking bastard," he sighs.

I shake my head and reply, "Yeah, I don't think you'd be saying that if he was your girlfriend's brother and he has a problem walking into her apartment whenever. Without knocking, I might add."

"Did he catch you two in the act?" Jake asks.

"No but he was probably close to it," I reply. "We were half dressed and eating breakfast."

Burns sighs again and tells me, "I still think you are one lucky bastard."

I shake my head and skate back out to warmups. I just want this game to be over so I can talk to Eliza.

This game is kicking our asses. The refs keep calling shit plays and that just means we are beating ourselves up even more.

I think I might break my sin bin record this game, because I sure am spending a lot of fucking time in it. Though I'm not the only one on the team, which makes me feel slightly better.

Every time I get to our box, I have to hold myself back from turning to look at Eliza. A few times I can just barely hear her yelling at the refs to do their jobs. At some point I realize that our first home game this season, it was Eliza yelling at the refs. I shouldn't be surprised, she's not afraid to tell you what she thinks.

"Put me in coach," I can just barely hear her say at one point. "I may not be able to skate, but I can do better than these idiots."

I bite my lip and try and focus on my teammates, waiting to get back on the ice.

Twenty minutes and I can see my girl. I just have to hold it together and keep my head in the game until then. As much as I want to think about Eliza being here I can't let my mind go there yet, we have a game to win.

CHAPTER 32
ELIZA

As soon as the game is over, I try to make my way to the tunnels as quickly as I can, but Zeke has other plans.

"What the fuck do you want Z!" I hiss.

"Where are you off to in such a hurry?" he responds.

I groan and say, "I'm trying to go talk to my boyfriend if you must know."

"Why?" he asks, knowing full well that he is pushing my buttons.

I give my dad a look and he just shrugs.

"If you're gonna ask questions then just come with me, but don't get in my way." I look at my dad. "You don't have to wait on me, I can catch a ride."

My dad responds, "Alright, kiddo. Love you, Liz."

"Love you," I say and turn back to Zeke to find a smug grin on his face. "Come on dick face, be the cock block that you are."

With that I head towards the tunnels, not caring if Zeke is behind me or not. I'm fully prepared to leave him behind if he doesn't follow or keep up. I'm many things, but my brother's keeper is not one of them.

I love my brother, I do, but I seriously question a lot of his actions. I sometimes think it's a miracle that the both of us have made it to adulthood.

We are waiting close enough to the locker room that we'll be visible to Remy when I ask Zeke, "Seriously Z, what were you doing here tonight?"

He looks at me and replies, "I told you dad invited me."

I give him a look that tells him I don't believe him.

He throws his hands up. "Seriously Liza. Dad invited me, and I had the night off and decided I wanted to spend it with my family. It's not that deep."

"But you don't watch hockey," I say matter-of-factly.

"Yeah, I know, but I can still want to support your boyfriend," he replies as if it's nothing.

"You've only met him once," I tell Zeke.

"So? You've never been this way about anyone, and I think it's safe to say that he's really fucking good for you."

"You know you're actually a pretty decent brother when you want to be."

"Hey, you and I are for life," he says. "Just in a completely different way than you and Miller."

I roll my eyes.

I look back up to find Remy coming out of the locker room with damp hair from his shower, and I can feel the smile taking over my face. He locks eyes with me and yells something back into the locker room.

He quickly jogs over and wraps me up into a hug. Immediately I wrap my arms around him and sink into his embrace, taking in all of him.

Zeke coughs and asks, "What am I, chopped liver?"

I roll my eyes as Remy lets go of me.

He sticks his hand out to my brother and says, "Good to you again, man."

Zeke takes his hand and replies, "Good to see you with more clothes on this time."

I smack him across the chest as Remy lets out a laugh.

The locker room door busts open, and four players come barreling out. I recognize Jake and Grant, but I don't know the other two.

Remy looks over his shoulder and groans.

"I'm sorry about this," he says to Zeke. "They found out you're Liza's brother and won't shut up about it. Especially Axel. Jake already knew, though he just likes giving me shit."

Zeke lets out a laugh and replies, "It comes with the territory. I'm just glad it's athletes, so at least they understand."

Remy nods before Zeke jogs over to Remy's teammates to start talking to them.

"So, your teammates are fangirling over my brother," I tease.

Remy looks at me and replies, "I still think you're the more famous Fox twin."

"Flattery only gets you so far," I say as I tease the hem of his shirt. "I'm not a household name like Zeke."

"You are to me."

The things this man says to me, I swear.

He smiles down at me before his lips are one mine.

I pull Remy closer by the hem of his shirt as his hands go to my hair.

"I missed you, so fucking much," Remy breathes as he rests his forehead against mine.

I smile and reply, "I fucking missed you too."

He kisses me again before asking his earlier question, "How are you here?"

He moves his hands to cup my cheeks and my hands move to his wrists as I reply, "I took this thing called a plane. Really Nash, you should try it sometime."

His eyes get a mischievous glint to them as he says, "Ha ha, smartass."

I smile up at him.

Remy's eyes fall to my lips before he says, "I'm gonna punish you for that later."

"Oh no," I fake concern. "Does that mean I've been a bad girl?"

Remy replies, "Keep going and you're going to give me a raging hard on, baby, and I can't have that in front of those dick-heads over there. They'd never let me live it down." Knowing full well that he's already half hard.

I give him a mischievous smile. In return he just gives me a look that tells me he dares me.

I let out a moan.

Remy groans and says, "Jesus Christ, Eliza."

He smashes his lips to mine, this time with more fire, and I can feel Remy adjust himself before pulling away.

"Do you want to be a good girl and properly answer my question?" he asks as his hand reaches around to cup the curve of my ass, pulling me that much closer.

"Hm," I pretend to think. "No. I think I want to be a bad girl and see what my punishment will be."

Remy pinches me, making me jump slightly before saying, "Wrong answer Eliza."

I smile up at him and reply, "I wanted to surprise you, so I booked an earlier flight without telling you."

"Best surprise," he says. "Who picked you up from the airport?"

I move my hands to his stomach as I answer, "My dad."

"You have no idea how happy I was to see you in the stands tonight," Remy says as he buries his face in the crook of my neck, and wrapping his arms around me once more.

"Yo love birds!" Zeke calls over to us. "Y'all want to grab some food with us?"

I look over Remy's shoulder to see Zeke pointing towards Remy's teammates.

I look back to find Remy looking at me and I say, "It's up to you babe."

"I'm starving," he replies.

I tilt up and whisper in his ear, "You can eat me out all you want later. I feel if we don't go Zeke will bother the shit out of us."

"It's the way I know you're dead serious about him doing that," he replies before turning towards them. "Yeah, we can go for some food."

Remy grabs my hand and leads me over to the group.

"Eliza you already know Grant and Jake," Remy points out. "This is Misha and Axel."

"Nice to officially meet you," I say. "I've only ever known y'all from the crowd."

They laugh at that, and we head out to our vehicles to head to the diner on Peachtree boulevard.

CHAPTER 33
REMINGTON

think I made a mistake agreeing to come eat with the guys rather than just taking Eliza home. One because I really fucking missed my girlfriend and am dying to make her come. Preferably on my face, but I'm not picky. Two because not only are my teammates totally freaking out about Zeke, but also because Zeke is being a typical older brother to Eliza. I mean that in the way that he's annoying the shit out of her, and I would know because I've don't the same thing to my sisters when I've been in the presence of guys they've dated.

"I swear if you fucking touch my milkshake, I'm going to fucking kill you, Ezekial," Eliza says as Zeke tries to steal a sip of her shake.

"Oh, come on Liz," he replies. "Just one sip, that's all I'm asking for."

"No," Eliza says, holding her ground. "First off it's mine, and second I will not be on the receiving end your nutritionist's fury, again."

I let out a laugh as Zeke tries giving her puppy dog eyes. I have a feeling that it usually works in Zeke's favor, but I don't see Eliza backing down.

"Just one sip."

"No. One sip will be half my shake, dickhead."

"For you older brother?"

"You're ten minutes older," Eliza replies.

Axel eyes bug out of his head as he asks, "Wait the two of you are twins?"

Eliza looks at him and says, "Sadly. Can't you tell the differences?"

"Wait," Jake questions. "Are you identical?"

Eliza and Zeke turn to look at each other and I can only assume that some kind of silent twin conversation transpires between the two, because no words are exchanged but they seem to be on the same page.

Eliza turns back to Jake and replies, "Honestly can't you see it?"

"Yeah, "Zeke chimes in. "Even our dad has problems telling us apart."

I hold back a laugh, because this is definitely something they've done before.

"Wait, really?" Jakes asks.

Eliza levels a look at him and says, "No. Male/female twins can't be identical."

Zeke pretends to wipe a tear away as he laughs. "Oh, dude you should see your fucking face."

Jake's jaw drops a little and Eliza busts out laughing, falling into me as she does.

Zeke takes the opportunity to try and steal a sip of her shake, But Eliza moves faster. She pulls the cup away while simultaneously slapping Zeke upside the head.

I hold back a laugh and pull Eliza closer.

"Can I have a sip?" I ask her.

Eliza hands me her milkshake and I watch Zeke's jaw drop as I take a sip.

"How come he gets some?" Zeke practically exclaims.

Eliza shrugs and replies, "What can I say? The man knows the way to my heart and how to make me come."

Zeke makes a gagging sound, and I snort out a laugh causing some of the shake to end up coming out my nose. Much to my dismay I know the guys are laughing at me and taking pictures. Honestly, I don't even care, because I turn to Eliza to find her smiling at me as she snaps a picture. I just know it's going to end up on her story, but I can't even be mad about it.

I lean close to her ear and whisper, "Do you want to be punished later?"

Her smiles turns mischievous as she quietly replies, "Maybe."

I pinch her side, and she laughs.

Eliza grabs a napkin and helps me clean up the spewed milkshake.

"Ratatouille," Jake says. "That was epic."

"At least it wasn't a Coke," Eliza replies. "That shit burns. And yes, I speak from experience."

Zeke lets out a laugh and says, "Remember when you spit your Coke all over dad's truck because you were laughing at him for trying to clean his windshield when it was below freezing?"

"He was cleaning Coke out of his dash for months," she says through a laugh.

I smile and take the time to think about my life. I have four friends on my team and am slowly starting to consider them more like brothers. I have an amazing girlfriend that I can genuinely see a future with. I know I'm in love with her, I just haven't worked up the courage to tell her yet.

I tune back into the conversation as Eliza is saying something to Axel.

"It's kinda weird that you're fangirling over my brother," she says. "Even though I should be used to this kind of shit."

He shrugs and replies, "Maybe to you, but to me he's one of the best tight ends in the country."

Eliza raises an eyebrow and says, "Yeah and I've been hearing that he's 'the best' since we were kids."

I smile hearing the faint hint of her accent coming through.

"You know Eliza's pretty famous herself," I pipe in.

She elbows me and replies, "No I'm not."

I look down at her and say, "Your name is in the credits of a ton of different movies."

Misha almost spits his sweet tea and exclaims, "No shit?"

I bump Eliza's knee with mine before replying, "Yeah. Y'all know my favorite movie *Down Comes Night?*" They nod. "Well, my girl here is responsible for editing it."

"Damn Ratatouille," Jakes gapes. "How the hell did you manage that?"

Eliza shrugs and says, "I'm just glad that my friend, Athena, trusted me to put it together."

I've noticed that Eliza usually puts more credit on the director or whoever else on the crew rather than herself. I love her for it, but I also think that she deserves her own recognition. The films she's worked on wouldn't be the same if someone else had edited them.

"Shit Eliza," Grant says looking up from his phone. "You've worked on a lot of good stuff."

"I believe they're looking at my IMDB page," Eliza subtly whispers to me, and I nod.

Grant passes his phone to Jake, Misha, and Axel and they take a minute to scroll.

"When does your next film come out?" Misha asks.

Eliza scrunches her face in thought before replying, "Um *Waterloo* comes out December 19th."

My friends share a look with one another before Grant says, "We'll be there."

Eliza's eyes almost bug out of her head as she replies," Y'all don't have to do that."

Jake waves her off.

"We want to," Misha tells her.

Axel adds, "The least we can do is go out to support you when you are at pretty much all of our home games. Plus, we see how you and Remy are good for each other. And I can't speak for the others but I kind of like you."

There are murmurs of agreement as Eliza's cheeks turn a light shade of pink.

"Thank you, guys," she says. "It means a lot."

Jake replies, "Of course. We've got our own movie star."

Eliza shrugs under my arm and replies a little sheepishly, "Yeah well my IMDB page doesn't show all the phenomenal short films that I've worked on as well."

"She's always been insanely creative," Zeke adds. "Growing up she was always forcing our dad and I to do something in her videos."

"I was channeling my inner Spielberg," Eliza says.

I smile at that, especially knowing that it's her absolute dream to work with the famous director.

"Have you ever thought about directing?" Misha asks, genuinely curious.

"Nope," Eliza replies quickly. "Directed one thing for a class I had to take and immediately knew that was not for me."

"*One Card*, right?" I ask before I think about what just came out of my mouth.

Eliza whips her head towards me and says, "Stalker."

"Sorry," I reply as my cheeks heat a little. "I saw it that day you started following me."

"And you got onto me and your sisters for doing the same thing."

I roll my eyes and shake my head. "That was different."

She squeezes my thigh and teases, "You're not really helping your case here, Nash."

"Wait, what's the story behind you calling Remy Nash?" Zeke asks.

Eliza gives a look and says, "That's none of your business, Ezekial."

He throws up his hands as I reply, "It's my first name. Everyone outside of my family has always called me Remy."

As I look around the table, Eliza is the only one that isn't remotely surprised that the name I go by isn't actually my first name. It's weird how people treat the knowledge of knowing your true first name, because you never know how they are going to react.

"Okay seriously y'all," Eliza says, and her accent comes out heavily this time. "Don't act like y'all ain't ever met someone that goes by their middle name rather than their first. Or hell I know plenty of people that go by their first *and* middle name."

"Where did you say you were from again?" Jake stupidly asks.

"I didn't," Eliza replies. "But I'm from bumfuck nowhere, Georgia."

Jake says, "I've never heard of it."

I close my eyes to stop from giving him a look. I swear Jake doesn't always know when to shut up and read the room. I know that Eliza is joking and being sarcastic, but Jake can't seem to pick up on that. I'm just glad that Eliza doesn't take offense to it.

Eliza pinches the bridge of her nose and tells him, "Well no shit Sherlock. It's not the actual name of it."

"It's literally the middle of nowhere," Zeke adds.

Man, I fucking love this girl.

"So," Grant expertly changes the subject. "Any plans for Thanksgiving?"

"My brother is coming to town," Misha replies.

"Are you excited about that?" Eliza asks him.

Misha nods and replies, "Yeah. I don't get to see him much since he is also an NHL player, and our schedules rarely line up."

Eliza smiles and says, "That's nice."

There are nods of agreement around the table.

Zeke pipes up after a few seconds and says, "I don't know what the love birds have planned but I know *I* have a game on Thanksgiving, and then I'm going up to my dad's the day after."

"We haven't had a chance to really discuss it yet," Eliza tells the group.

After that we all fall into easy conversation. I'm impressed with how easily Eliza and Zeke fit in with my friends; it makes me feel good about our relationship.

CHAPTER 34
ELIZA

SUPER GRAPHIC ULTRA MODERN GIRLS

CAMILA THE NOLAN WANNABE

I'm in town for a few days bitches. Let's meet up

ATHENA GODDESS OF WISDOM

I'm down

ME

Just tell me where and when

CAMILA THE NOLAN WANNABE

Yes my beautiful bitches! Let's fucking go!

Remy tightens his hold around my waist and buries his head between my breasts. Krypto jumps up on the bed next to me and curls up in the crook of my arm.

"What if I just never let you go?" Remy asks.

I run my fingers though his hair and reply, "Then my friends would lead a search party for me. And you really don't want that."

"Fuck that," he says, and I smile. "You're mine."

"Don't you have things to do today before your game tomorrow?" I ask.

He sighs and rolls off of me.

I pat his cheek and say, "Good boy." I look to Krypto. "I'm sorry buddy but if your daddy has to get up, then so do you."

"When can I meet your friends?" Remy asks me.

I freeze. I've not thought about that because he's met all the other important people in my life.

"Um," I start. "I guess whenever you have a chance, and they are in town. I'd have to talk to them first."

Remy nods and replies, "Good. I've met your family, and you've met my friends. I want to meet yours."

I love this man more and more every day. I should tell him soon, but I also don't want it to feel like it's too soon. Of course he wants to meet my friends, I guess it's really the only next logical step in our relationship.

I move my arm from around Krypto and he yells at me. I pick up him and cuddle him for a minute before setting him on Remy's chest.

"How come I don't get loves like that?" Remy pouts.

I lean over and kiss him but pull away before we get too distracted.

"Better?" I ask as I run my fingers up and down his stomach.

Remy moves his hands behind his head as he flexes his ab muscles.

"I know of something else that needs your attention," he says as he winks.

I trail my hand down his stomach and dip it under the covers that are pooled at his waist, and a palm his hardening dick. I give him a squeeze and lean forward.

"If you're a good boy today then I'll take care of you later," I tell him before releasing him and getting up.

Remy slaps my ass before grabbing me around the waist, causing Krypto to jump off his chest.

His hand goes to squeeze one of my breasts and says, "You're such a tease."

He releases me and pinches my ass as I walk to get my clothes.

I turn to find him back lounging on his bed, with a hunger in his eyes. Remy watches my every move as I get dressed.

"You're obsessed," I tease.

He smirks and replies, "You're damn right I'm obsessed with you Eliza Grace Fox."

I pull my shirt on and crawl up the bed to Remy. I straddle his waist, and he places his hands on my thighs.

"On a scale from one to ten, how obsessed would you say you are?" I ask leaning forward and crossing my arms on top of his chest.

His hands move to where my thighs meet my hips and he squeezes as he says, "I'm gonna give you my last name one day, obsessed."

"Who says I don't want to give you my last name?"

He quickly flips up so he's on top and I instinctually wrap my legs around his waist. Remy settles between my legs before saying, "If that's what you want baby, then I'll gladly take your last name."

I love you, I think, but bite my tongue so it doesn't come out. Instead, I pull him closer and smash my lips against his.

Remy's hand moves under my shirt, and he rubs back and forth on my hip.

I break our kiss even though it's the last thing I want to do. Remy groans and I smile knowing he feels the same way.

"Nash," I say. "I really need to go."

He dramatically rolls off me onto the bed and replies through a sigh, "Fine."

I roll out of his bed and start towards the bedroom door.

"Eliza," he calls out from the bed.

I grab the door frame and turn to look at Remy.

"Yes?" I ask.

"I love you," he says.

I feel my eyes widen and before I realize what I'm doing I'm bolting through the living room in an attempt to get to the front door.

Fuck! What the hell am I doing?

I force myself to stop at the front door and take a deep breath. I stand there for a minute before realizing how bad it must look to Remy that I fucking ran away when he told me he loved me.

Releasing the doorknob I turn to run back to him only to find Remy coming around the corner with a pair of sweat pants hung low on his hips.

I don't think before throwing myself at him. Remy catches me and I wrap my legs around his waist. My hands go to either side of his face as I fervently smash my lips to his.

Remy shifts and press my back against a wall.

"I'm sorry," I say as I trail kisses down his jaw. "I don't know why I ran. I wasn't expecting you to say it."

He tucks one of my curls behind my ear and replies, "It's okay, Eliza. If you're not ready to say it then I'll wait."

"I love you," I say, moving back to his mouth and one hundred percent meaning the words I just uttered. "When I'm not with you I feel like I can't properly breathe, and then I see you and everything's okay again."

I kiss him again and this time it feels different, almost as if we're savoring the moment.

"I never thought that I would need someone as much as I need you Eliza," Remy tells me. "I feel like the luckiest man to be able to call you mine."

What in the world did I do to deserve this man?

I tilt my hips trying to find some friction when my phone rings.

"Hello," I answer.

"Bitch where the fuck are you?" Athena asks.

"Liz I'm here before you," I hear Cam say.

Remy opens his mouth to say something, but I put a finger to his lips.

"Seriously, you're always habitually early to everything!" Athena exclaims.

Remy nips at my finger and I give him a look.

"I got sidetracked," I reply as my eyes lock on his.

Cam pipes up, "I bet she's getting fucked ten ways to Sunday."

"She would be if I was having my way with her," Remy says, his deep voice full of lust.

"Oh my god," I hear Athena say. "I didn't think you'd actually be fucking him right now."

"Oh shit, seriously?" Cam asks.

I sigh and reply, "No he was kissing me goodbye. But I wish we were in bed."

Both Athena and Cam practically squeal.

"Like I said," I tell them. "I got sidetracked.

Remy smirks at me and I lightly smack his chest as I roll my eyes.

"I'll be there in ten," I tell my friends before hanging up.

Remy steps back from the wall and sets me back on the floor, while sliding me down his body.

"You sir," I point a finger up at him. "Are in so much trouble for that."

He has the audacity to smile at me and say, "I'm looking forward to what my punishment is going to be."

"Masochist."

"Only for you baby, only for you."

"Yeah, yeah whatever," I say. "I love you and I'll see you later.

Remy presses one more kiss to my lips before replying, "I love you too."

I smile and head out the door before I fall back into bed with Remy.

CHAPTER 35
REMINGTON

When I told Eliza that I love her I didn't expect her to run away. I know I really shocked her when I said it, I honestly shocked myself. For a minute or two I really felt the blow to my heart as I watched her run away. I truly thought I had blown one of the best things in my life just by telling Eliza that I love her. Thankfully when I went to the living room she was still there, and literally jumped into my arms to profess her love for me.

I desperately needed to be inside her after our confessions, but Eliza's friends called, and she had to go.

I'm about to get in the shower and take care of my hard on when my phone rings. I let out a groan.

"Hello," I answer, sitting on the edge of my bed.

"Hi Nash," Georgia says. "I just want to make sure that you're good to watch Max later."

Fuck. I forgot that I agreed to watch my nephew. How the fuck did I forget that?

"Yeah," I reply. "I'm still good to watch my favorite nephew."

Georgia says, "Nash, he's your only nephew."

"So? What I said is still true."

I can hear her roll her eyes as she asks, "Will Eliza be joining us for Thanksgiving?"

Eliza and I finally had the chance to talk about our plans, and we figured that there was no reason we couldn't visit with both of our families.

"Yeah," I say. "She'll be here when y'all come over Thursday for lunch. Then we'll go to her brother's game, and Friday we'll go up to her dad's house."

I get up from my bed, no longer hard, and head towards my fridge.

"I'm so glad that I finally get to meet her," Georgia says.

"As if you and Ari haven't been Insta stalking Eliza since you found out about her," I reply pulling some stuff out to make a late breakfast.

"Yeah, but that's different."

"You're just lucky my girlfriend is just as crazy as you and Ari," I say putting my phone on speaker. "She stalked the both of you after you followed her."

"Oh Nash. That's just how us women are."

I roll my eyes. "Do you have an idea of what time you'll be dropping Max off?"

"After lunch?"

"Georgia!"

"What! I just want to have time for myself. You know I don't get to have this often."

I let out a sigh and say, "Yeah that's fine."

"You're the best big brother a girl could ask for."

"I'm your only brother."

"Exactly, anyways see you then. Love you."

"Love you too."

She hangs up and I turn to Krypto.

"Well buddy," I tell him. "I guess Maxie is coming earlier than we originally thought."

He just meows at me and that pretty much sums up how I'm feeling at the moment.

To make myself feel better I finish making my breakfast and head to the living room.

Krypto jumps up on the couch next to me as I sit down, and I turn on *Down Comes Night*. I watch in the new light that Eliza is responsible for editing this film, and it's kind of like she's here with me.

As I watch the movie, I realize that I would love to pick her brain about this film sometime, especially since she said it was, her friend Athena's passion project. I love hearing how Eliza talks about her friends films, and that she gives them more credit. I'll make sure Eliza receives the credit she deserves one day, even though I have the feeling all the directors she's worked with give her plenty of credit. I just want Eliza to give herself the credit she deserves more than anything.

CHAPTER 36
ELIZA

When I walk into the Mellow Mushroom, I immediately see Cam and Athena sitting in a booth near the back. It's honestly kind of hard to miss Cam when she dyes her hair bright colors all the time.

Athena waves me over and I slide in next to Cam.

Cam elbows me in the rib before exclaiming, "You sneaky bitch! I can't believe you would try and abandon us for some dick."

I try holding back a smile but fail spectacularly.

"I wasn't getting any dick, thank you very much," I reply as the waiter comes over to take my drink order.

Athena coughs as the waiter walks away and says, "Yet. You weren't getting any yet."

Cam throws out a hand and exclaims, "Exactly! Who's to say what you and your man would have gotten up to if we hadn't called."

I lean back and let out a laugh. "Your just jealous I'm regularly getting good dick."

Our waiter sputters as he sets down my drink and quickly walks away to possibly compose himself before getting our food orders.

"See what you've done Cam?" I joke. "You made that poor man uncomfortable."

Cam fake gasps and replies, "I did no such thing. That was all you, bitch."

I drop my jaw like I'm offended and Athena steps in, "Now, now ladies. Cat fight later. Right now, we need all the details."

I roll my eyes.

"You want details," Cam starts. "But I want to know when I get to meet the son of a bitch who thinks he can claim by best friend's heart."

They both look at me expectantly.

I throw up my hands in mock surrender and say, "I don't know what you're talking about."

Athena rolls her eyes and Cam lets out a loud groan.

"Liz don't play that game with us right now," Athena levels at me. "Seriously, when can we meet Remy?"

I sit there for a minute before replying, "You know he was asking me the same question before I left."

"Was this before or after he was mauling you?" Cam asks.

I give her a look and reply, "Ha, ha. Very funny. It was actually before I even made it out of bed."

"That doesn't answer my question," Cam says, and I know she's just trying to stir shit right now.

"Who said that Remy was trying to maul me in our bed?" I ask, feigning innocence.

I watch as both of their jaws drop in pure shock.

After a few seconds Athena says, "I love when dirty mouthed Eliza comes out to play."

Cam dramatically throws her head back and replies, "Why are you only like this when you have a man? We haven't seen this side of you since Xander."

I shrug and nonchalantly tell them, "I have no idea what you're talking about. I'm always like this."

It's Athena's turn to level a look at me before saying, "I expect this kind of thing from Zeke, but not you."

"You been talking to my brother?" I ask, teasing her about her very obvious crush as her cheeks turn pink.

"No," Athena sputters. "The only time I talk to him is when the two of you are with each other."

"We're rarely together," I say. "And I'm nothing like Z."

"Uh huh," Athena replies.

"To be fair when y'all are together the two of you are like one unit," Cam points out.

"Can we go back to talking about my boyfriend and his amazing dick?" I groan, trying to steer the conversation back to something else.

Athena's eyes light up as she exclaims, "Ah hah! So, you admit he has a good dick."

I slide down in my seat a little. I hate every part of this.

"Never said it wasn't," I reply.

Cam pinches my side and says, "Oh come on Lizzie. Denial is not a good look on you."

I roll my head to the side and smirk at them.

"Oh my god," Athena exclaims. "Fucking look at her Cammie!"

My smirk widens as I say, "A girl doesn't suck and tell."

They both let out a loud squeal and I bite my lip in an attempt to keep my smile from growing.

"Oh, now we've really got to meet the bastard," Cam replies. "Just tell us when."

I think on it for a moment before replying, "Next time both of you are in town. I'll make sure that the three of you meet. There's just a lot going on with it being Thanksgiving."

"As long as we actually get to meet him," Athena says.

"Why wouldn't you?" I ask. "I genuinely see a future with Remy, and he wants to meet y'all. So really, it's only inevitable."

"Because we haven't met anyone since Xander," Athena says.

"There's been *no one* to meet," I reply. "Y'all don't want to meet one-night stands."

Cam takes a sip of her drink and says, "True that. Then they get clingy."

"Gross," I reply. "I promise though, Remy is one of the good ones. I've accidentally met his friends, and Remy has already met my dad and Zeke."

Cam's jaw drops as Athena spits out, "Oh shit. You really are serious about this guy."

I pull out my phone and unlock it.

"Girl what the fuck was that picture?" Cam practically shrieks in excitement.

I was going to show it to them anyways, but I decide to let them see Remy's Instagram post he made when the picture was taken.

I hand Cam and Athena my phone and their eyes practically bug out of their heads.

"Oh Remy," Athena starts. "I was not aware of your game."

"Hot damn!" Cam exclaims. "Damn Eliza, you've got it bad if you asked him to do this."

"Yeah," Athena chimes in. "I know this is something that you've wanted to recreate with someone for a while, but you never felt like you could ask."

"Yeah, the Johnny Depp crop top and the Spider-man kiss, those are the dream," I say.

"Do you think Remy would be willing to do the Spider-man kiss?" Athena asks me.

I look at her and honestly reply, "If he can get upside down."

"Why are you both so hot?" Cam whines.

I look at her and reply, "Bitch, you're hot too."

"Yeah, but not this hot," she says turning my phone back to me. "Like damn. Have you ever licked anything off these abs?"

I give them a small smirk and tuck a piece of hair behind my ear.

Cam gives me a shove and exclaims, "You bitch! You kinky bitch! I can't believe you aren't flaunting this more."

Athena coughs and says, "Cam you know Liza isn't one to flaunt anything."

I raise an eyebrow and tell Cam, "Sweetie you wouldn't know kinky if it bottomed out in you and made you come so hard you saw God."

I tuck another piece of hair behind my ear smile as I watch their reactions. Athena's jaw drops so far, I think it will hit the table. Cam practically spits out her drink. I love catching them off guard like this.

"Thank you, Remington Miller, for bringing back this version of Eliza!" Cam praises.

I shake my head and say, "Thena pick your jaw up. You'll catch flies otherwise."

Her jaw snaps shut, and she shakes her head at me.

"Welcome back," Athena replies. "The true version of Eliza has been missed."

"Yeah, yeah, don't cream your pants," I dryly respond.

I can't remember the last time the three of us were able to sit down and chat like this. Between Cam and Athena being busy upcoming directors and me being in an editing booth a lot, there's not much time for us to just chill together. Our group chat is rarely dry, but being with my friends in person is something else, especially when the three of us play off of each other like we are now.

We easily spend three hours sitting there shooting the shit with each other, and just catching up in general.

My phone dings in my pocket and I pull it out to see that Remy texted.

NASHVILLE <3

Can you come over? I need help

ME

I'll be there in ten

I have no idea why he needs my help, and this doesn't seem

like a true SOS situation otherwise he would have sent that instead.

"Everything okay?" Athena asks, reading whatever passed over my face.

"Yeah," I say, putting my phone back in my pocket. "Remy just said he needs help. So, I should probably get going."

"Maybe it's just code for he needs to be inside of you," Cam suggests.

"Nah. If it was that he would've just said so," I tell her and start to stand up.

Cam replies, "Even with people around?"

I shrug. "Why try innuendos when you can be direct? Anyways I'm so glad we got to do this."

"Same," Cam and Athena reply in unison.

"I'll see y'all later," I say and turn to walk away.

"Tell Remy we said hi!" Cam exclaims.

"Until next time Eliza!" Athena calls out. "Aur revoir bitch!"

I roll my eyes and flip them off as I walk out the door to head towards Remy's apartment wondering what he needs help with.

CHAPTER 37
REMINGTON

When it gets close enough to lunch time, I go around my house picking up everything that Max could potentially get into. I love the little guy, and while he's almost three he is a complete mess.

Just as I'm getting the last of my stuff put away there's a knock on my door.

I open it and smile down at my nephew, who is in my sister's arms.

"There's my favorite guy," I say holding out my hands for him to come to me.

He immediately comes to me and exclaims, "Rex!"

"Hey Maxie," I say. "You ready to spend your day with me?"

He nods enthusiastically.

I look to Georgia and tell her, "Have fun, and don't do anything I wouldn't do."

"Yeah, yeah, whatever *dad*," she replies.

"Say bye to your mom, Maxie."

"Bye Momma," he says.

Georgia tickles Max and replies, "Be good for Uncle Rex, okay?"

With that she turns to leave, and I shut the door, leaving me and Max alone.

Setting him down I ask, "Alright Maxie, what do you want to do first?"

"Cars!" he practically yells.

I give him a big smile as he grabs my hand and leads me into the living room. The two of us get comfy on the couch and I pull up *Cars*. I know this likely won't keep his attention long, but it's a start. I'm just glad this is one of my favorite movies, otherwise I'd probably get bored of it with how many times Max has seen it. Though when I think about it, I guess it is kind of my fault that the kid is obsessed with this movie.

"Rex?" Max asks after a few minutes. "You play on tv?"

"Yeah Maxie," I reply. "My games are on the tv."

"We see you play?"

I nod and say, "You're going to see me play tomorrow."

This seems to satisfy him for now because he turns back to the tv and continues watching.

By the time the credits roll I can tell that Max is fighting going to sleep.

"Do you want to take a nap?" I ask him.

"No," he replies.

"Max, you need to nap," I tell him.

He crosses his arms and pouts. "No Rex. I not tired."

I pinch the bridge of my nose, knowing this is not going to be an easy battle.

"Please Max," I say. "For me?"

Max shakes his head and replies, "No."

I pull out my phone and shoot a quick text to Eliza.

ME

Can you come over? I need help

Her response is almost instantaneous.

THE FUTURE MRS. MILLER

I'll be there in ten

"Do you want to watch another movie?" I ask and he shakes his head. "Are you hungry?"

"No." Max faces away from me.

I sigh. "Come on Maxie, you gotta work with me here bud."

"No, Rex."

I'm thankful when I hear a knock on my door and mentally make a note to give Eliza a key.

"So, what do you need help with?" she asks when I open the door to let her in.

I point towards Max and say, "Him."

Eliza glances that way and her eyes widen as she asks, "Oh my god, do you have a kid?"

I quickly shake my head and reply, "No. Max is my nephew."

"Phew," she says. "Sorry. If he was yours, I was going to ream you out for hiding him for so long. I knew you had a nephew, but couldn't be sure if you had a kid or not when I've never met him."

I let out a laugh.

Eliza rounds the couch, and I stand back to watch the interaction.

She squats down in front of Max and gently says, "Hi, I'm Eliza. What's your name?"

I watch as he turns his head towards Eliza and shyly tells her, "Max."

She smiles and asks, "Do you have a favorite movie, Max?"

He turns fully towards her and exclaims, *"Cars!"*

Eliza smiles and replies, "That's a good one. Do you want to be like Max Verstappen?"

"Who's that?" Max asks, hanging onto Eliza's every word.

She lets out a fake gasp and says, "Only one of the best drivers on the European Circuit."

"Why not the fisin cup?" he asks meaning the Piston Cup.

I have to admit she's got me intrigued and I have no idea if this person is real or made up.

"Because they're afraid he'll steal Lightning's title."

Max gasps, and I move behind the couch.

"That's why he has to race the European Circuit," Eliza says. "He drives really fast, and a lot of people don't like him for that."

"Why?" Max asks.

"I don't know," she says. "I guess the same reason Chick doesn't like Lighting."

"But he's *Lightning McQueen!*"

"I *know.*"

Eliza looks up at me and smiles.

"You know this guy?" she asks as she points up at me.

Max turns and looks up at me before turning back to Eliza and saying, "That's Rex."

She smiles, and I see Eliza mentally file that away.

"Well let's see if Rex has a piece of paper and a pen and I'll make a deal with you," Eliza replies. "Does that sound good?"

Max nods and I grab a pen and a piece of paper for her.

She takes them and says to Max, "Alright if I draw Lightning McQueen for you, do you promise to do what Rex asks of you?"

I can practically see Max bouncing in his seat.

"Otay," he replies.

Eliza holds out her pinky and asks, "Pinky promise?"

Max wraps his pinky around hers and she shakes it.

When he lets go both Max and I watch in amazement as Eliza draws a damn good Lightning McQueen for my nephew. I guess she wasn't joking when she said she originally wanted to be a Disney animator.

Eliza puts down the pen after a couple of minutes and turns the picture towards Max.

"Max, can you tell me what Rex was asking of you?" she asks, not yet giving him the picture.

I can see his lip start to tremble as he replies, "He wants me to take a nap."

"Why don't you want to take a nap?" Eliza asks gently.

Max shrugs.

"Can I tell you a secret?" she fake whispers and waits for him to nod. "There's nothing wrong with a nap. I take them and so does Rex."

Max looks at me for confirmation, and I nod in agreement.

"Will you take a nap now?" Eliza asks.

When he nods, she passes the drawing to him, and he gladly picks it up.

"Do you want Rex to put you down?" Eliza asks.

Max shakes his head and replies, "No, Iza."

"Okay squirt," she says and reaches to pick him up. "You want to go to Rex's bed?"

Max nods and curls up against Eliza's shoulder.

I sit on the couch and watch as she takes him back to my room.

She comes back out a few minutes later and crawls up me and rests her head on my chest.

"I didn't think he was ever going to go down," she says, muffled in my chest.

I wrap my arms around her and reply, "I'm sorry. Georgia mentioned a while back that Max loves saying no, I guess I just didn't realize that also meant refusing to nap."

"Glad I could help," Eliza says.

"You're probably going to become his favorite person now that he knows you can draw Lightning McQueen."

"I can also draw Mickey Mouse, Minnie, Goofy, and a bunch of other characters."

"Don't tell Max that or you'll never stop."

Eliza lets out a laugh.

"It's a cool party trick, huh?" she asks.

"Yeah, if you're a kid," I reply jokingly.

She pinches my side, and I tighten my arms around her even more.

"You're lucky I love you," she says.

I smile. "Say it again."

"You're lucky—"

I cut her off with a kiss and say, "The other thing."

She smiles and replies, "I love you."

I smile and tell her, "I love you too, smartass."

I kiss her again, but we don't go any further with Max just down the hall.

After a few minutes I ask, "Who is Max Verstappen?"

Eliza buries her face in my chest as she lets out a short laugh.

"He's a driver in the Formula 1 circuit," she replies. "He races for Red Bull."

"So, he's a real person?" I ask.

She fails at holding back a smile before asking me, "Did you think he was fictional?"

I pinch her sides and reply, "I wasn't sure. I wouldn't have been surprised if you had made him up on the spot for Max."

Eliza smooths her hand over my chest where my heart is and says, "I'm good, but not that good. Especially when it comes to someone like Max Verstappen, you just have to see him drive to understand. They don't call him the Flying Dutchman for nothing."

I smile and kiss her lips lightly.

"Let's watch a race the next time one is on."

"Babe, I love that you want to do that, but COTA and Vegas have already passed. Which means that we would have to get up at like eight in the morning or earlier to catch one of the two remaining Grand Prix's live."

I furrow my brow trying to figure out what the hell COTA is, but thankfully Eliza can read me like a book.

"Circuit of the Americas. It's the race in Austin, Texas," Eliza supplies.

I nod and lightly kiss her again before asking, "How do you know all of this?"

"My grandfather loved watching any kind of races, and I would watch a lot of them with him just to spend time with him," she replies. "Z knows a lot about different kinds of races as well."

"I fall in love with you and your brain more and more every day," I say.

"But you only told me that you love me today."

"That doesn't mean that I haven't loved you for longer."

Eliza smiles and presses her mouth to mine. Both of us are extremely conscious of not taking things further with Max sleeping down the hall, and I don't need Georgia giving me more shit than normal.

"I love you," Eliza slightly whispers.

"I love you too, Eliza Grace," I reply and wrap my arms around her, holding her closer.

CHAPTER 38
ELIZA

ater that day, after we have exhausted the little gremlin from playing all day, Remy and I fall asleep on the couch not long after putting Max down for the night. The thing is I just didn't realize I'd fallen asleep until I am startled awake and falling to the floor. I lay there staring up at the ceiling for a second as I try to gather my bearings.

Remy leans over the side of the couch and asks with sleep still heavy on his voice, "Why are you on the floor?"

Before I can answer the knocking that originally startled me starts up again. Remy groans and grabs his phone off the coffee table as he runs a hand down his face and through his hair.

"That'll be Georgia," he says.

Sitting up on the couch he holds out his hands for me, I take them, and he pulls me close as he wraps his arms around my waist. I knot my hands behind his neck and play with the ends of Remy's hair.

"Nash we should answer the door," I say, running a hand through his hair.

I might have a slight obsession with his dark silky hair.

Remy buries his face in my stomach and replies as he tightens his arms, "I know."

I shake my head and he reluctantly let's go. He lets out a sigh and pushes to stand up.

As we walk towards the door Remy wraps and arm around my shoulders and tells me, "Just prepare yourself, okay?"

I look up at him and say, "You know you have met Zeke. How much worse could Georgia be?"

"Trust me babe," Remy replies. "You just have to experience her for yourself."

I raise an eyebrow at him as he opens the door to his sister, Georgia.

"What the fuck, Nash?" she asks as she barrels through the door. "What took you so long? I was about to send out an amber alert."

Remy looks at me as he shuts the door and says, "She wouldn't actually, she's just dramatic as fuck."

"Again, you have met my brother," I reply. "And I wouldn't be surprised if Georgia did actually send out an amber alert for Max just because we didn't answer the door fast enough."

I watch as Georgia's head whips toward me.

"Oh my god!" she exclaims. "Hi, I'm Georgia. I didn't realize you were here, Eliza." At that she shoots Remy a pointed look.

"Your son loves saying no," Remy says, feigning innocence.

I elbow him and reply, "It's nice to officially meet you, Georgia. I've heard a lot about you."

She smiles and says, "Likewise. Now back to my son."

Georgia gives Remy a look and he shrugs as he answers, "Maxie didn't want to go down for a nap, so I had to call in reinforcements. And he only recently went down for the night."

He pulls me to his chest, and I reply, "And by reinforcements he means my drawing abilities."

Remy leans down and says, "To be fair I didn't know that you could do that."

Even though Remy can't see I wiggle my eyebrows and joke, "Yeah well I just have a way with the guys."

Georgia lets out a laugh as Remy pinches my side.

She meets his eyes and says, "What did I tell you?"

Curiosity piques my interest, and I ask before Remy can say anything, "And what did Georgia tell you Nash?"

Georgia's eyes widen as she replies, "Oh I was so right. Wait till I tell Ari."

Remy groans before grumbling, "That I was going to fall in love with you and be so fucking whipped."

"I didn't quite catch that. Can you repeat yourself, Nashville?" I ask sweetly.

Georgia practically squeals and says, "Nash seriously, Eliza knowing your full name tells me everything I need to know."

I glance over my shoulder and tell Remy, "What did you say?"

He narrows his eyes and replies, "Georgia said early on that I was going to fall in love with you and be so fucking whipped."

I pat his cheek and say, "Good boy."

Remy squeezes my side and replies lowly, "You're going to be punished for that later."

"Can't wait."

Georgia breaks our bubble by saying, "Oh Ari is going to ecstatic when I tell her."

Remy groans and replies, "Please don't."

"Now, now big brother," Georgia lilts. "I wouldn't be your baby sister if I didn't torment you."

"Don't you have your son to pick up?" Remy deflects.

Georgia waves him off and heads towards his room to get Max.

"Never let her and Zeke meet," I whisper. "I fear if they do, we'll never know peace again."

Remy groans again. "It'd likely be the end of the world if they meet."

Georgia comes out of Remy's room with Max who has apparently just woken up as he cries, "Iza!"

I walk over to them and say, "It's okay Maxie, you've got your mom."

He looks up at me and says, "My McQueen!"

I grab the drawing and show him and reply, "Don't worry he's right here."

Max grabs the paper and seems to go back to sleep.

Georgia mouths to me, *Thank you.*

I nod and follow them to the door with Remy.

"Will you be at our Thanksgiving?" she asks, though I feel like she already knows the answer to that.

I nod and reply, "Yes, and if y'all are at the game tomorrow then I'll likely see you there as well."

Georgia nods and says, "Good. Thank you, again. Both of you."

Remy closes the door behind his sister and nephew and pulls me into a tight hug. He rests his chin on the top of my head as I wrap my arms around his waist.

"Have I told you I love you lately?" he asks.

"Mmm. I don't think so," I reply. "Might as well do it now just to be safe."

His arms tighten around me as he says, "I love you."

I lift my head from his chest and kiss the underside of his chin before replying, "I love you too."

Remy moves his arms to my legs and lifts me up. I immediately wrap my legs around his waist, and he takes me to bed.

CHAPTER 39
REMINGTON

let out a breath. I hadn't really been thinking when I got the tickets for my family, and I sure as hell hadn't thought to run it by Eliza to begin with. Which was fucking stupid on my part, because what if she wasn't okay with that?

I let out a laugh. It still manages to surprise me how well Eliza and I know each other, especially in the short amount of time we've known each other.

After she'd left this morning to try and start getting ready for Thanksgiving it had been weighing on me to tell her that her and Jeremiah would be dealing with my family tonight.

THE FUTURE MRS. MILLER

Seriously Nash, stop overthinking it. I know it just slipped your mind

ME

How the hell do you do that?

THE FUTURE MRS. MILLER

What?

ME

Read me like a fucking book, Eliza Grace

THE FUTURE MRS. MILLER

I like to think it's my crazy awesome girlfriend powers

ME

Ha ha

THE FUTURE MRS. MILLER

But also I think it's just cause we get each other on a different level

ME

But you're seriously ok with it?

THE FUTURE MRS. MILLER

It's either meet them at the game or Thanksgiving. I'm not going anywhere anytime soon

ME

Damn right. You're my future Eliza Grace

I wish I could see her face as she read that.

After a few minutes I assume that she isn't going to say anything, but my phone buzzes with a new notification. I smile at seeing her name.

THE FUTURE MRS. MILLER

Ok. I do have a question. Not related to families

ME

Shoot

THE FUTURE MRS. MILLER

Have you ever done a flying v?

The *fuck*?

ME

The hell is a flying v?

THE FUTURE MRS. MILLER

Well in nature birds fly in a v formation when migrating south for the winter. In hockey it's when the ducks form a v behind their goal to skate toward the offensive zone together

I read what she wrote again before responding.

ME

Like the Tampa Bay Ducks?

THE FUTURE MRS. MILLER

Well technically they were the mighty ducks before, because the Disney company wanted to expand into sports after the movie of the same name came out.

They only changed the name to the Tampa Bay Ducks after the team was sold

I let that information soak in for a minute. I didn't realize Eliza knew trivial stuff like that.

ME

1. Never seen The Mighty Ducks 2. Didn't know you had facts like that ready to go

THE FUTURE MRS. MILLER

We'll come back to the mighty ducks thing in
a sec

I have a lot of weird facts stored up in my brain
for no reason. Do you think that's hot?

ME

Extremely. Just don't spit them out when I'm
going down on you

THE FUTURE MRS. MILLER

Don't worry I won't be spitting out random
serial killer facts while you are making me come
on your face

Only thing I'll be spitting out is your name 😊

I'm choosing to ignore her comment about serial killers, for
now. That's a question for future me.

ME

Damn right

THE FUTURE MRS. MILLER

Rewind. What the fuck do you mean you've
never seen The Mighty Ducks?!?

ME

THE FUTURE MRS. MILLER

Have you seen Miracle?

I let out a scoff.

ME

Of course. I feel like it's a right of passage every
American hockey player needs to go through if
they want to play for an American team.

THE FUTURE MRS. MILLER

> *wipes sweat off brow* good. I thought I was going to have to break up with you

> Tomorrow night we're going back to my place and fixing this problem

I almost forgot that my girlfriend is a big movie buff outside of working on them.

I look *The Mighty Ducks* up and see that it's streaming on Disney+.

ME

> It's on Disney+. We could watch it at my place.

THE FUTURE MRS. MILLER

> Nope

> VHS is the only correct answer to experience it for the first time

ME

> Yes ma'am

I think for a second.

ME

> Is this an all time favorite for you?

THE FUTURE MRS. MILLER

> Oh yeah, easily top 4 on letterboxd

ME

> What are the other top movies?

There's no hesitation in her response.

THE FUTURE MRS. MILLER

Back to the Future (obviously), Shrek, The Mighty Ducks (duh), and Batman: Under the Red Hood

ME

That's a wide variety of films

THE FUTURE MRS. MILLER

What can I say I'm versatile

ME

Ok but who still has VHS tapes though?

I know the answer even before I sent that, but I love seeing how Eliza reacts to things.

THE FUTURE MRS. MILLER

I do, because I love movies and physical media is better. That's like asking an audiophile why they prefer vinyl over digital

I've seen some of her physical media collection already, so that's not surprising. Which causes me to let out a laugh, because she does have a point.

THE FUTURE MRS. MILLER

Don't get me wrong, I love the convince of streaming, but nothing beats the crackle of a VHS tape when you out it into the VCR

ME

Be kind, rewind

THE FUTURE MRS. MILLER

Man I fucking miss Blockbuster

I try doing the mental math to figure out if Eliza was even old enough to know what Blockbuster was.

ME

Do you even remember Blockbuster?

I realize it's the wrong the to ask after sending it, but I can't take it back because Eliza has already read it.

THE FUTURE MRS. MILLER

Of course I remember Blockbuster. I'm 25 Nash

Going to the theater to see something was a treat growing up. So we ended up at Blockbuster most Fridays. Z and I could each pick a movie

ME

Sorry it slipped out before I thought about it

THE FUTURE MRS. MILLER

This is a text chain

ME

My fingers were moving before my brain could think

THE FUTURE MRS. MILLER

Ima let it slide for now. But you, me, popcorn, and The Mighty Ducks tomorrow night

ME

It's a date

THE FUTURE MRS. MILLER

I love you, see you at your game tonight

ME

I love finding you in the stands with the number 26 and MY last name across your back

THE FUTURE MRS. MILLER

> Maybe I should wear my Ramirez jersey as your punishment

I let out growl. I should burn that fucking jersey, but I won't because I know it holds significant value to Eliza.

THE FUTURE MRS. MILLER

> That made you jealous didn't it? Maybe made you growl a little

> That's one thing you never have to worry about babe, I'm yours & only yours

Fuck, Eliza knows just what to say to me.

ME

> Damn right you are

THE FUTURE MRS. MILLER

> See you at your game tonight Nash 

> I'll be one of the Foxes sitting with a bunch of Millers

ME

> Can't wait to see that

With that I get up to start suiting up to walk into the arena.

To say I'm excited might be a bit of an understatement. My girlfriend is getting to meet my family, and it really cements how I feel about this woman.

CHAPTER 40
ELIZA

"Remy's family is going to be sitting with us," I tell my dad as we sit in our seats.

"The more the merrier," he replies with a smile.

I let out a small sigh and say, "I told him you'd say that."

Dad lets out a small laugh before asking me, "And how do you feel about it, baby girl?"

One thing about my dad is he never shied away from making sure that Zeke and I felt comfortable talking about our feelings with him. Our birth giver decided to leave all of us, so dad always made sure that he was there for us for everything.

I look at him and say truthfully, "I was going to meet them tomorrow anyways. I don't know, it's just been a while since a guy wanted me to meet his family."

I know what I told Remy yesterday, and it wasn't a lie, I am okay with meeting his family today. But like I told my dad, I genuinely haven't had to meet a guy's parents since I was with my ex.

My dad nods. "That just means Remy is serious about you, bug."

I nod and turn back toward the ice. Warmups will be starting soon, and I am ready to watch my boys play some hockey.

"Iza!" I hear Max yell.

I turn to see him coming down the stairs to our seats. He looks so cute in his mini jersey and vans.

"Hey Maximillian!" I exclaim and hold out my arm. "How's my favorite race car driver?"

"Good!" he practically yells. "Mommy's going to put my McQueen on my wall!"

"She is? That's awesome!"

I look up from Max to see Georgia smiling at us. I move my eyes to the others around her. I find Arizona looking at me with a similar look, and next to her is a man—I assume is her husband—with light brown hair and brown eyes. Behind them is an older couple I assume to be Remy's parents. Looking at both of them I can see a mix of them both in Remy, but he definitely favors his father. At least I know that Remy won't be ugly as an older man, if anything he'll age like fine wine.

"Hi," I say to the group.

"Eliza," Georgia replies. "This is my sister Arizona, her husband Calvin, and my parents Virginia and John."

"It's so nice to finally meet you, Eliza," Virginia says to me. "I see you've already met Max."

I smile and reply, "Yes ma'am. I met him yesterday."

My dad lets out a cough.

I look at him and say, "I didn't forget you. I'm trying to use the manners you taught me. I'm not like your son." I turn back to the Miller family. "This is my father, Jeremiah."

The Millers take their seats as the team comes out for warmups.

I spot Remy as he comes out of the tunnel and point him out to Max, "There's Rex."

The kid is literally bouncing in my lap at seeing his uncle.

"Do you want to go to the glass?" I ask Max.

"Yes!" he vibrates.

I quickly glance at Georgia, and she gives me a short nod.

I scoop Max up and carry him down to the glass as Remy

skates over to us. He smiles first at Max, and his eyes lock with mine and I can feel the smile pulling at my lips.

"Rex!" Max exclaims.

Remy looks back at Max and holds up a finger. He skates over to grab a puck and comes back to us. As he stops in front of us again as he tosses the puck over the top of the glass. I catch it and hand it to Max.

I smile as his little eyes light up and how he looks back at Remy. Max squirms a little, telling me he wants down. I set him on the floor, and he runs back to his family.

When I look back at Remy, he's staring at me with such love in his eyes. I place my hand on the glass, and he puts his on mine on the other side.

I love you, he mouths.

I love you too, I mouth back. *Now go win this game for us.*

He smiles and shakes his head before skating away to warm up.

I'll never tell Remy this, but I really enjoy watching warmups for the sole fact that the way the players stretch is almost sexual. The goalie stretches might just be my favorite, but Remy is forever my favorite player.

CHAPTER 41
REMINGTON

My heart is practically busting at seeing Eliza carrying Max down to the glass to see me. From the way he's taken to her you would never know that my nephew only met my girlfriend yesterday. Funny how he was the first of my family to meet Eliza.

When I skate back over to Jake, I can still feel the smile on my face, and I really don't care about the shit the guys will give me for it. They don't know what it's like to be in love like this.

"You're like a lovesick puppy," Jake teases.

"Oh, shut up," I reply. "You won't be saying that when you have a woman of your own."

Grant skates over and ribs, "Yeah Smitty here will never settle down."

"Hey!" Jake exclaims. "Well, you're not entirely wrong."

I shake my head and reply, "Just know there will be a big 'I told you so' from me the day you finally do settle down."

"So, the kid?" Grant starts. "He yours or something?"

I let out a cough and say, "Jesus, you're the second person to think that. Why?"

Jake answers, "The kid has a strong resemblance to you."

I turn my head to look at Max. I guess I can kind of see what Jake is saying, but I don't really at the same time.

"I mean he is my nephew," I reply. "My baby sister's kid." I point Georgia out to them.

"Dude is she single?" Jake asks. "Cause she's an absolute knockout."

I elbow him in the stomach, hard.

"That's my fucking sister," I say through gritted teeth.

I sure as hell am not going to tell him if Georgia is single or not, I feel Jake doesn't need to know. I know him and I know my sister. Georgia is someone that would rather date longterm, and Jake fucks like there's no tomorrow.

Grant lets out a sharp laugh and I shoot him a glare. He holds his hands up and skates off to go stretch.

I'm passed a puck and take a shot on goal. When the puck hits our goalie's glove, I skate away to let someone else at it.

I shake out my limbs. I feel really good about this game. Honestly it doesn't really matter the outcome—okay it does— but I have not just my family here but also my girlfriend. I feel that tonight is going to be good.

When we head back into the locker room before puck drop, I'm approached by Madi, one of our rink side reporters.

"Hey Miller," she says with a smile. "Can I grab you for a quick interview?"

I nod my head.

Honestly, I could say no and just pay the fine, but since I've been on the team our media team has pretty much left me alone, which is weird since I'm new to the team. I feel I can give them one short interview.

When Madi gets the all clear she starts her introduction.

"Good evening, Flames nation!" she says with a professional smile. "I'm here with right winger Remington Miller." She turns toward me. "How have you been adjusting to the team?"

I lean my chin on the top of my hockey stick and reply, "Honestly pretty well. Since I was traded the rest of the guys have treated me like I've been here since day one."

"How are you feeling about the game against the Ducks tonight?" Madi asks.

I say, "If we go out there and play like we I know we can, then I don't think we'll have a problem. At the end of the day if we're able to say we gave it a hundred percent, then there's not much we can complain about."

She nods. "Okay last one, and this is only to please the people."

I have a feeling where this is going and nod.

Madi starts, "Is there anything special about the fan you gave a puck to? That's not something you often do."

I still cringe a little, even though I knew the direction the question was going, and I'm so fucking glad that Madi tried to word it the way she did.

I rub my chin and say, "Yeah, my girlfriend brought my nephew down to see me. I love having him here, especially since he doesn't get to see me play in person often."

Madi smiles and replies, "Thank you, Miller."

When she's given the cue that the camera is off, she turns to me.

"I'm so sorry about that," she says. "If I didn't ask, I'd get chewed out."

"It's okay," I reply. "Thank you for wording the question nicely."

She sighs as she says, "It's the least I can do. You know how the fans can be."

I nod.

"I gotta get to the locker room before coach chews me out."

"Go," she waves me off. "And good luck!"

I smile and reply, "Thank you."

I turn toward the locker room and take off in a jog.

CHAPTER 42
ELIZA

This game has been anything but boring, but then again hockey is never boring to me. My dad always says that we come to a fight to see a hockey game break out, and I think that's very fitting for this game.

So far both teams have spent a good amount of time in the penalty box, and we are barely into the second period. Call me weird, but I love seeing fights at a hockey game, almost more than the sport itself. Something about a good hockey fight just absolutely changes the energy in the arena, and I love it.

The Flames steal the puck from the Ducks and are skating towards their goal quickly. The puck is passed to Remy, and he rears back to take the shot. Just as he gets it sent off one of the Ducks players crosschecks him. Remy stumbles back and the Ducks player mouths something off to him before I see Remy dropping his stick and gloves.

In one motion Remy has the Ducks player grabbed by the jersey and starts pounding into him.

I jump to my feet like the rest of the crowd and cheer the fight on. I don't even notice that another fight has broken out until Remy and the Ducks player hit the ice before the refs pull the two off each other.

Now I know Remy is no stranger to the penalty box, but I've found that he doesn't get into a lot of fights. So, whatever the Ducks player said to him definitely set him off enough to throw the first punch. I make a mental note to ask him about it later.

As the referees pull the two players off each other, I'm still on my feet like the rest of the crowd as they're led to their respective penalty boxes along with the second offenders.

I can feel the smile on my face from witnessing the fight, and it only grows wider when Remy's eyes lock with mine. I can see a little bit of fear in his eyes, but when he sees my expression, it quickly turns to smug satisfaction.

So hot, I mouth to him.

I see the glint in his eyes as he walks into the box. He sits down and I pull out my phone to snap a quick picture of him.

I put it on my Instagram story, tag Remy, and write the caption, "came to a fight and a hockey game broke out. Weird huh?"

Remy squirts some water into his mouth and watches the game. I can see him restraining from looking back at me, which I think is fucking hilarious.

I lean over to Max and whisper, "Go bang on the glass next to Rex."

He immediately does and Remy turns to look at Max before turning to look at me.

Remy raises an eyebrow at me as Max comes back to his seat. I just smile and shrug. Remy shakes his head and turns back to the game.

With only a few seconds left of his penalty, he gets up and waits to be let out. He immediately goes to the bench, and locks eyes with me. Oh, I can feel we are going to have fun when we get home tonight.

CHAPTER 43
REMINGTON

The sun streams across my face the next morning and I pull Eliza closer. She lets out a groan and curls into me.

We ended up winning five to three last night, but honestly, I wouldn't have cared if we lost after seeing the look on Eliza's face after my fight. I was so afraid that she would look down on me for fighting, but when I looked up at her she was smiling like a lunatic. I sometimes forget that she was a hockey fan long before she ever met me. I'm pretty sure Jeremiah was yelling "hit him again."

Last night I learned that my girlfriend has a thing for hockey fights and apparently being covered in my own blood turned her on which led us to go back to my place rather than hers because it was closer.

When I had gone to the locker room at the end of the game, I saw she had tagged me in something on her Instagram story. When I opened it up, I laughed so hard at it, reposted it on my own story, and showed a nagging Jake, who also got a good kick out of it.

I'm honestly excited for our Thanksgiving meal later today, which is something I haven't been able to say in a while. My family will be coming over for lunch, then after Eliza and I will head to the Benz for Zeke's game later today.

My family has been extended an invitation, but they decided they were going to head back home and beat the traffic. Which is totally fine with me, especially because they are more hockey people than football people. Though I know they wouldn't complain about it if it meant that we were spending time together.

Eliza wraps her arm around Krypto, and he chirps. I swear I think my cat likes my girlfriend more than he likes me. Though I can't blame him, she is pretty fucking great.

I kiss Eliza's shoulder, and she presses her ass into me. I can feel my cock hardening.

"We need to get up, baby," I say and kiss her shoulder again.

She groans and presses against me harder. I lightly thrust my hips into hers.

Eliza's eyes snap open and she mumbles, "We can't have sex in front of the baby."

She roughly gestures to Krypto and I let out a laugh as I tighten my arm around her waist.

"Then let's get up," I suggest.

Eliza throws her face into her pillow and replies in a muffled voice, "Let's go back to sleep."

One thing about Eliza is that she is not a morning person. She's such a night owl, but it's also a struggle for her to get up early. Eliza once told me that she's always been like this, and that she's a really heavy sleeper, which is something I've learned the hard way. She said it's one of the things she likes about being an editor because she rarely has any early mornings.

"My family will be here in a couple of hours," I tell her as I tickle her side.

Eliza shrieks and kicks me, when she settles down, she says, "Damn you and your good looks."

I smile and tease, "Are you calling me pretty?"

She turns and looks at me. She grabs my face and pulls me down to her lips.

"You're more than just pretty," she says, breaking our kiss. "You're fucking hot." Another kiss. "And so fucking handsome."

My hand moves to her waist, and I squeeze as she kisses me long and slow.

Krypto butts his head against my arm.

I rest my forehead on Eliza's and say, "The child wants to be fed."

Eliza plays with my hair as she replies, "Our child, Nash."

Fuck. I like the sound of that, even if Krypto is just a cat.

I smile and tell her, "I like the sound of that."

"Good, cause I'm not going anywhere anytime soon. Plus, I think Krypto kind of likes me," she says as she gets up.

I turn onto my back as I watch Eliza leave my room in nothing but her underwear and my shirt.

"Come on Toe," I hear her say to Krypto. "Let's get you some food."

I smile at her words. She has some strange nicknames for Krypto, and even me, but I genuinely have no idea how she comes up with them. But I love every one of them.

CHAPTER 44
ELIZA

When the doorbell rings my stomach is in knots. I know it makes no logical sense why I'm nervous because I met Remy's family last night, but I also know that this will be more one on one.

Remy squeezes my shoulders as we walk to the door.

"Hey," he says turning me to face him. "There's nothing to worry about. I know for a fact that they already love you."

"But they barely know me," I reply.

Remy lifts my chin so my eyes meet his before telling me, "Yeah, but I can't seem to shut up about this amazing woman that's somehow stolen my heart. And they are somehow good judges of character"

I shake my head at him and turn to open the door. On the other side stands Remy's family, all with warm smiles on their faces.

Max launches himself at my legs, just about taking me down but luckily Remy reaches out and steadies me.

"Hi Iza!" Max beams up at me.

"Maximillian!" I reply as I start to tickle him. "How's my favorite race car driver?"

He squeals.

Remy smiles and jokes, "Am I just chopped liver to you now, Maxie?"

Max looks at his uncle and tries to tackle him.

"Rex!" Max yells.

"Oof," Remy says. "Keep this up kid and you'd make a great defensive lineman."

"What's that?" Max asks.

Remy opens his mouth, but I beat him to saying, "It's a position in football. They try to stop the other team."

I step back to let the Millers in so they aren't just standing in the hallway. Remy also moves, along with Max.

Remy stares at me.

I shrug and say, "What you think I'm just a hockey fan? I'm also a football fan."

"No, I know," Remy replies. "I just forgot that you would know a lot about it."

I let out a laugh as I take a plate from Georgia and start towards the kitchen and say, "Nash, my brother is a tight end for the Atlanta Ravens. I grew up on SEC football, in a football household. I only became a fan of hockey a few years ago."

I set the plate down on the counter and Remy's jaw gapes a little. I smile at seeing him trying to keep his attraction to me in check.

"What's SEC?" Max asks.

I look down at him and reply, "College football. Do you know what college is?"

He shakes his head, and I take his hand leading him to the couch.

"It's like school for really big kids," I say.

Max's eyes light up and he replies, "Woah."

I hear Remy's dad let out a short laugh and tell Remy, "She has you there, son."

I smile as Georgia and Arizona sit down next to me.

"I'm surprised Remy hasn't said anything about your brother

being a pro athlete," Georgia says, and I can see a glint in her eyes that I can't quite read.

Arizona shakes her head and replies, "It's not really that surprising, seeing as he only talks about Eliza here."

"Well, I just meant in the fact that she has experience with pro athletes," Georgia tells her sister.

Arizona meets my eye and says, "I'm sorry about her."

I wave her off and reply, "My brother is the same way. Just be glad none of y'all had to share a womb."

"Iza?" Max asks. "Can you do another McQueen?"

"Of course, buddy," I tell him with a smile. "Can you ask Rex for paper and something to draw with?"

Max eagerly nods and bolts off to the kitchen where Remy and his parents are getting the food plated.

"Wait you're twin?" Georgia asks.

I let out a sigh. I'm used to it honestly, because it's a common reaction from people. Another common thing when people find out I'm a twin is asking if Zeke and I are identical, which is impossible.

"Yes," I say as my phone starts buzzing. "Speak of the devil."

I answer Zeke's facetime and before he can get anything out, I say, "Clean mouth dickhead, there's little ears present."

"Where are you?" he asks confused by my statement.

"My boyfriend's for Thanksgiving," I reply. "Say hi to Georgia and Arizona."

I flip my phone towards them and they both wave and say hi.

Out of the corner of my eye I see Georgia mouth something to Arizona, which causes her to elbow Georgia in the ribs.

I turn my phone back to me and ask, "What did you need?"

"Are you coming tonight?" he responds.

I roll my eyes and say, "Z, this could've been a text, or you could've just asked dad. I'm also ninety percent sure we've already had this conversation."

He gives me a smug smile and replies, "I know, but I like hearing it from my baby sister."

I huff. "I'm ten minutes younger, and Remy and I will be there with dad."

"Was that so hard baby sister?"

I give him a look and say, "Bye."

I toss my phone on the coffee table after hanging up and let out a sigh before telling Georgia and Arizona, "I swear he always does this. Things that could be a text, he either shows up at my place or calls me."

"It's nice to know all older brothers are shit heads," Arizona says. "Though Nash isn't as bad as he was when we were younger."

Remy carries Max back into the living room and the youngest Miller asks, "What's a shithead?"

Georgia smacks Arizona and exclaims, "Ari!"

Arizona shrugs and says, "Sorry?"

I let out a laugh and tell Max, "A bad word, Max. One that your aunt didn't mean to say."

Max giggles and Remy puts him down.

"I don't even want to know what you three have been talking about in here," Remy says and leans down to place a kiss on my head. "Also, lunch is ready."

"Let the feast begin," I say as I rub my hands together, causing laughter from the Miller siblings.

"So, Eliza," Virginia says later on. "Nash tells us you work in film?"

I nod as I swallow my bite of food and reply," Yes ma'am."

She smiles and asks, "How long have you been in the industry?"

"I've been working in the film industry for four years now," I say. "But I've been working on films since high school."

John asks me, "What exactly do you do in the film industry?"

Remy squeezes my thigh as I reply, "I'm an editor. So basically, I take all the footage and turn it into the final story the audience ends up seeing."

"That's actually really cool," Georgia says.

Remy smiles and tells them, "Right? Eliza worked on *Down Comes Night* as the lead editor."

"Isn't that one of your favorite movies, Nash?" Virginia inquires.

Georgia rolls her eyes and says, "Mom you know he never shuts up about it."

Remy ignores her and replies, "It is. So, imagine my surprise when I found out."

I wave him off and say, "*Down Comes Night* was my friend Athena's passion project, and I'm just glad she chose me to help bring her baby to life."

Athena loves all the movies that she's directed, but *Down Comes Night* will always hold a special place in her heart.

Remy nudges my shoulder and tells me, "That movie wouldn't be what it is if it wasn't for you. Own that babe."

I smile at him.

I've noticed that he does stuff like that a lot, making sure that I get plenty of credit for the work I did. I love him even more for it.

Conversation flows easily, and surprisingly it feels like I've always been a part of this group. I'm so used to the dynamics of a group to feel stilted and awkward at first, but not this one. I think it helps that the ice was broken last night at the game.

I can tell that Remy really loves his family, and they love him. It's nice to feel like I'm already part of the family.

When it is time for them to leave, I almost feel disappointed, which is not something I usually feel when it comes to stuff like this.

As Remy closes the door after his family finally leaves, he turns to me and asks, "What now?"

I look at the time.

"Now we get ready to go to my brother's football game and

then we go back to my place to watch *The Mighty Ducks,* since we didn't get to it last night," I say as I smile up at him.

Remy pulls me close and says before kissing me, "I kinda thought you would've forgotten about the movie."

I narrow my eyes at him and reply, "How dare you think that Nashville Remington. Shame on you."

He laughs as he kisses me again.

"My bad," he says between kisses. "I should never think you'll forget about movie plans."

I smile and reply, "Damn right. Movies are my love language."

Remy laughs again. "I thought food was your love language."

"That's the way to my heart."

"Oh right, my bad."

My smile widens as I look up at him and Remy tugs me toward the bedroom, since we have time before we need to leave for Zeke's game.

CHAPTER 45
ELIZA

Surprisingly Remy made it through all of *The Mighty Ducks* last night. I'm used to him crashing way before one in the morning if he can help it.

Not surprisingly, he really enjoyed *The Mighty Ducks*, but who doesn't like a good underdog story. We plan on watching the other two after this next stretch of away games and when he's not at practice.

Remy's arms tighten around my waist, and he says with a gravelly voice, "I know you're awake Eliza Grace."

I scoot back into him and rub my ass on his quickly hardening dick.

His arm tightens more, and he growls, "You're playing a dangerous game if you aren't going to follow through."

I make a humming noise and rub up against him again.

"Will you punish me if I'm a bad girl?" I ask as Remy teases the top of my shorts.

I can hear the grin in his voice as he replies, "You already know the answer to that sweetheart."

Even though he can't see my face I feel a wicked grin take over my face. I act like I'm playing with his hand before pulling it off of me and slipping out of bed.

I hear him groan and I school my features as I say, "I'm getting in the shower."

I start the water and mentally start counting to see how long it will take Remy to join me, because I know he's not going to let that slide.

I'm fully in the shower and coming up on two minutes before the bathroom door closes. I smile as I watch him quickly strip out of his boxers and open the shower door to join me.

"That wasn't very good girl of you, Eliza," Remy says shutting the door, and crowding my space.

I smile up at him and reply as I run a finger down his chest, "And what if I told you I like when you punish me?"

He groans and leans an arm on the shower wall, "Jesus fucking Christ."

My smile widens as he brings his mouth down to mine.

My arms wrap around his shoulders and one of my hands tangle in his hair. Remy moans as I tug on his hair and his hands wrap around my thighs to lift me up. I wrap my legs around his waist, and I feel his cock nudge my entrance.

"Nash," I groan.

Remy pants, "I don't have a condom."

I shake my head and say, "I'm on the pill. And I'm clean."

"Me too," he replies. "Are you sure baby?"

"Yes," I tell him. "I want to feel you."

A shiver runs through Remy's body as he says, "Just to warn you, I don't know how long I'll last like this this first time."

I gently caress his cheek and reassure him, "I don't care Nash. I just want to come on your dick with nothing between us."

I see the hunger in his eyes as I say that. Remy nods and lines himself up with my entrance before thrusting up into me. I tip my head back against the shower wall and let out a moan.

I roll my hip trying to get some friction and Remy says, "Goddamn baby. You feel so fucking good but keep this up and I really won't last long."

"Fuck me Nash," I reply breathlessly.

He rolls one of my nipples between his fingers and asks, "What's the magic word?"

He quickly thrusts in and out and stops.

"Please," I beg breathlessly. "Fuck me Nashville."

He smiles and starts moving his hips. His hand trails down my body and circles my clit. I can feel my orgasm slowly building.

I bring Remy's face to mine and kiss him like my life depends on it as he bottoms out inside of me.

I can feel my walls starting to tighten around him, and my pleasure building more at the base of my spine.

Remy grabs a handful of my hair and pulls my head back, so he has access to my throat. He lets out a moan as he sucks on my collar bone.

I know Remy is getting close, because his movements are getting jerkier, and his breathing is becoming uneven.

"Yo Liz!" Zeke yells from somewhere in my house.

My head snaps up and I stare at Remy as he stills. This is not the time for my brother to randomly show up.

What the fuck? I mouth to Remy.

He doesn't say anything, instead the bastard gets a mischievous glint in his eyes as he snaps his hips against mine.

Oh, it's going to be like that, I think. *Well two can play that game.*

"I know you're home," Zeke calls out, getting closer to my room. "So, where the hell are you?"

Barely suppressing a moan as Remy circles my clit I yell back, "I'm in the shower dickwad!"

I lean forward to bite Remy's collarbone to suppress another moan as he pulls all the way out just to slam right back into me. He seems to like that because he groans before pulling on one of my breasts into his mouth.

"What the fuck do you want?" I manage to yell to Zeke as Remy swirls my nipple with his tongue.

He looks up at me through his lashes and whispers, "I'm so

fucking close, Eliza, and your fucking brother isn't going to stop me."

"Me too," I whisper back breathlessly.

I think Remy might secretly like the idea of getting caught.

"Do you want to ride together to dad's?" Zeke asks, now in my room.

I'm so fucking glad that Remy closed the bathroom door, otherwise my brother would have a full view of my boyfriend fucking my brains out against the shower wall.

"That could've been a text," I say through a moan.

At the bathroom door Zeke asks, "Are you okay in there?"

I'm so close and I know Remy is too.

"Don't you fucking dare open that door Ezekial Gray!" I yell.

"Come on my cock, baby," Remy whispers. "Let's see how quiet you can be.

I'll take that challenge.

Zeke says, "It's not like it's not anything I haven't seen before."

I roll my eyes as my pleasure tips over and crashes through me. It takes everything in me not to yell out Remy's name. My hand goes to his hair, and I tug as his lips capture mine.

"I'm serious Z!" I manage to get out when my high comes down. "I'm fine. Now go to the living room, or your own home."

Remy's hips become more erratic, and I pray Zeke can't hear the sound of skin slapping skin over the water before I feel him filling me up.

He kisses my neck and says, "I fill you up so well Eliza Grace."

Remy holds my limp body to him and carefully pulls out. We both wince at the loss of contact.

Through lidded eyes I watch as Remy scoops his come up off my legs before pushing it back into me. He removes his finger and brings them to my mouth.

"Open for me," he says quietly.

I open my mouth and suck on his finger. He pulls them out with a pop and brings them to his own mouth.

"Wait," I hear Zeke say. "Isn't Remy going to dad's as well? Where is he?"

I don't say anything, I just watch Remy's almost black eyes as our chests move up and down together.

"Oh, what the fuck!" Zeke exclaims. "He's in there with you, isn't he?"

I smile, glad that he's finally getting it.

Remy pushes a wet curl behind my ear and kisses me. It's not as urgent as before; no, this kiss is slow and deliberate.

"I love you," he says.

I smile at him and reply, "I love you too."

"You were so good at being quiet, but I love it when you scream my name."

My smile widens and I say, "Only if you scream my name as loud as you need to sweetheart."

Remy carefully slides my body down his frame and pinches my ass.

"Tease," he says. "Now let me wash you off so we don't traumatize Zeke anymore."

On shaky legs I turn and reply, "It's his own fault. Remind me to change my locks so he can't do that again."

Remy laughs as he lathers his hands with my shampoo and tells me, "It was kind of hot thinking that we were going to get caught."

"Yeah, but I'm serious about changing the locks this time."

"As long as you have the key to my heart you can do whatever you want," Remy replies.

I sag against him and enjoy as much of the shower as possible.

CHAPTER 46
REMINGTON

When Eliza gets out of the shower, I'm honestly surprised that she is able to walk straight. I stand in the doorway of her shower and smirk at her as I watch her get ready.

Fuck. I can't believe she is mine.

She catches my eye in the mirror as she wrings out her hair with a towel before tossing said towel at me. I wrap it around my waist as I follow her naked form out of the bathroom. Luckily Zeke isn't in Eliza's room, otherwise that would be worse than it already is for all three of us. I guess he vacated the room quickly after realizing where I was.

Before Eliza can grab a clean pair of underwear, I turn her around and kiss her.

"Get dressed," she demands. "Our morning has been cut short."

I love it when she bosses me around.

"Yes ma'am," I reply before going back to the bathroom to brush my teeth, and to pee.

As I run my toothbrush under the water I take in my appearance. My eyes immediately zero in on Eliza's teeth marks where she bit me on my collarbone.

Holy fucking shit that had been so hot. I genuinely thought I was going to come just from that. I make a mental note to take a picture of the spot before the day ends. Because while that memory will stay with me forever, I also want the proof.

Eliza sticks her head into the bathroom. Her curls are still wet, it doesn't really look like the towel did anything.

Her eyes graze over me and she says, "You look like a man that's been thoroughly fucked, Nash."

I spit out my toothpaste and reply, "I am. And you babe, look so fucking sexy."

Even though she just has on a pair of jeans and a hoodie, Eliza will look like sex appeal in anything to me.

"Get dressed," she says. "The sooner we face Zeke, the sooner we get his tantrum over with."

Before she walks away, I grab her sleeve and pull her close to me.

"It's so worth it though," I tell Eliza as I kiss her again.

She pulls away, though I can tell that she doesn't want to.

Eliza looks up at me tells me, "Get dressed. I'm walking out of here."

And she does just that.

It doesn't take me more than five minutes to get dressed, and when I open the door to the bedroom, I hear the twins arguing.

I round the corner and Zeke says, "Agh he even looks smug walking around after doing whatever the hell he just did to you."

Eliza rolls her eyes.

I wrap an arm around her waist and plant a kiss on the top of her head before moving to the kitchen to get something to drink.

"How many times have I told you to knock because I could potentially have a guy balls deep inside of me?" Eliza asks.

I try to keep my smugness in check as Zeke fakes gags, or possible it's real. I'm actually not sure.

"I don't need to think of my baby sister having any kind of sex life," he shudders.

I watch as Eliza crosses her arms and pops her hip as she tells him, "At least I'm getting some, unlike you big brother."

Zeke gags again and asks, "Does your boyfriend really have to walk around smug about your heinous acts?"

Eliza glances over at me as I walk back to the living room, and replies, "This is our home."

That does something to me, hearing Eliza refer to her apartment as *our* home.

"I don't know what you're talking about Zeke," I say setting down my cup and taking a seat on the couch. "I'm walking normally."

Zeke dramatically flops back and exclaims, "My baby sister just got railed while I was on the other side of the door!"

"Title of your sex tape," Eliza quips.

My mouth falls open as I sputter, "Did you just—"

She cuts me off saying, "Pull a Jake Peralta? Yes, I did."

"I love you," I reply. This woman is my soulmate, I know it.

Brooklyn Nine-Nine is one of my favorite shows, I just wasn't aware that Eliza had seen it. I'm not surprised though; she loves movies and shows so much she wanted to be a part of what makes them happen.

She smiles at me and before she can say anything Zeke exclaims, "Ugh! Both of you are the worst!"

Eliza slaps his legs and sits down next to me, snuggling into my side.

Eliza says, "Oh shut up you big drama queen." She turns to me. "You would think I'd be the more dramatic one since I literally work in the film industry."

I let out a laugh and pull her closer.

As I've gotten to know Eliza—and even Zeke—I've come to know that Eliza can be dramatic. When together Zeke is like a golden retriever and Eliza has more of the black cat energy, but that doesn't stop her from being just as dramatic if not more than Zeke. Though I would never dare to tell her that, I do value living.

Eliza pokes Zeke with her toe and asks, "You want to get Waffle House before heading to dads?"

Zeke shoots up and says, "Hell yeah! And you're paying because you've traumatized me enough today, and I think you should pay for my emotional well being."

Eliza rolls her eyes and replies, "You didn't see anything." She smirks. "Or hear anything for that matter."

Zeke's hand's shoot up to cover his ears and loudly sings, "La la la la, I can't hear you."

I shake my head and pinch Eliza's side.

She looks at me and asks, "Waffle House good with you?"

"As long as I'm with you I'm good," I reply.

Zeke throws a pillow at us and says, "Get a room, you two."

"We had one," Eliza pulls my arm around her chest and reiterates, "Maybe you should learn to knock dickhead."

I know that if I don't step in these two will just keep going all day.

"What time do you want to leave?" I ask to no one in particular.

Eliza looks at her phone and questions, "Maybe nine thirty? Ten at the latest?"

Zeke replies, "Yeah that works."

And just like that the twins have momentarily forgotten about an argument that I suspect has been going on for most of their lives and will likely never cease.

CHAPTER 47
REMINGTON

Once we are all fed and on our way to Jeremiah Fox's house the twins surprisingly keep their arguments to minimum. Although at one point they did get into an argument about who would be driving. Eliza ended up winning and said and I quote, that I was her "passenger prince" today.

Since I've lived in Atlanta, I've never thought much about going out of the city. I don't know why, the farther away we get from inside the perimeter the more spaced-out things become.

It isn't until about an hour or so of driving north on I-85 that Eliza starts to get onto the off ramp, and I really realize just how little there is here. Not to say that this exit isn't busy, there just isn't much compared to other exits closer to the city.

As Eliza turns left at the light she tells me, "Growing up there wasn't much here. Maybe that McDonald's and Cracker Barrel."

Even though she says this area has grown up it still looks nothing like Atlanta, which is probably a good thing.

"Yeah, that Dairy Queen has only been there for like five or six years," Zeke points out on the left. "We used to have to go to Jefferson if we wanted DQ, before that one was built."

"Good old Braselton," Eliza says.

"It doesn't seem that big," I reply.

Eliza goes through a roundabout and takes the first exit as she replies, "Yeah, this part. The whole of Braselton goes across three or four different counties."

"Damn," I say as I watch the road, which looks less like an interstate exit. "It's still really beautiful out here though."

"If you want really beautiful," Eliza tells me. "I should take you to Tallulah Gorge or Amicalola Falls sometime, those are a couple of the prettier state parks."

Zeke replies, "Trust me, our Lizzie here knows her state parks."

"All because of dad," she says. "He took us to most all of them in Georgia growing up, did a lot of geocaching and camping. Also canoeing."

I smile. I can just imagine a young Eliza trekking through the woods with her dad and brother as they looked for said geocaches.

At the stop sign Eliza takes a right, and it's not long before we take another right into a driveway. A beautiful white house with a green roof comes into view.

"You weren't kidding about this being the middle of nowhere," I tell Eliza as she puts her Jeep into park. "I didn't realize that your dad's house would be surrounded by so much land."

"If you think this is great, you should see our uncle's place," Zeke says. "He's just down the road, but it's still family land."

My eyes widen as I look at Eliza.

She smiles and replies, "Come on, dad's probably wondering what's taking us so long. We can ride the property later if you're up for it."

Eliza grabs my hand as I round the front of her Jeep, and she leads me toward the front door.

Neither Eliza nor Zeke bother knocking, and for a second, I wonder if this is where Zeke gets it from. If I had to guess I would say that Eliza and Zeke grew up not knocking on their families front doors.

Jeremiah is kicked back in a recliner watching the University of Georgia versus Georgia Tech game.

"How are they looking?" Eliza asks, which surprises me a little, because I figured it would've been Zeke asking first.

Jeremiah sighs and sits up as he says, "You know how they've been playing this season."

Eliza closes the front door and moves toward the couch, with me in tow.

"Sobering up after halftime and only playing the second half?" she asks sitting down.

I sit down next to her and Jeremiah tells me, "Good to see you again Remy, I'm glad you could make it."

"Good to see you too, sir," I reply.

Zeke comes back from wherever he had gone and plops down into the other chair.

"At least they are somewhat playing," he says pointing to the game.

Jeremiah shrugs and Eliza replies, "If they're playing like last week then they've likely given up a couple of touchdowns or run the same play multiple times in a row thinking it would change."

Both Jeremiah and Zeke nod and I ask, "Dogs or tech?"

"We're go dawgs," Eliza replies with no hesitation.

I nod my head. Even though I'm not the biggest football fan I know the basics; you can't grow up anywhere in the south and not at least know a little bit about it. I also know that Eliza and her family are big on football, even if she and Jeremiah are also hockey fans now.

"Who's your team?" Zeke asks.

I think about it for a second before replying, "Um, I'm not sure. I really only know that Michigan has a pretty good hockey team."

Eliza pats my leg and says, "You're lucky you're pretty. We'll turn you eventually. UGA has a decent hockey team."

I actually didn't know that. With hockey not being that big

here in the south as other parts of the country it's not that surprising that I didn't know though.

Honestly, I'm cool with becoming a Bulldog fan if it means that Eliza is happy.

We continue to watch the game and it's interesting to watch Eliza become all animated like her dad and brother. I wonder if she gets like this at my games.

She catches my eyes and leans closer whispering for only me to hear, "You good?"

I nod and reply, "Yeah, just wondering what you're like when you're watching my games."

"A lot more into the game," she says as she rubs her hand up and down my thigh slightly. "A lot like this. Shit talking the refs, sometimes the players."

"I would love to see you in the audience at a hockey game."

"How about we got to an ECHL game one night when you're off?" she asks. "Then you can see for yourself, though it won't be the same not cheering for my favorite hockey player."

I kiss Eliza's forehead and say, "I'd love that."

"Fair warning though," Eliza warns. "The Glads aren't exactly the best in the league."

"That's okay. As long as I get to watch you, I'll be happy."

"Ugh," Zeke groans. "Dad please make it stop. I can't deal with those two anymore."

"Ezekial," Jeremiah replies. "Let your sister be. She's in love, maybe one day you'll find someone and be like that one day."

Eliza sticks her tongue out at Zeke, and I pull her closer.

The rest of the day we spend laughing and trading stories before we go out to eat.

By the time we start to head back I feel very content.

I'm even more cemented in the fact that I want to spend the rest of my life with Eliza, but I'm content to keep learning about each other until then.

CHAPTER 48
ELIZA

t's been over a week since I last saw Remy during the Thanksgiving holiday, and my hands and vibrator can only do so much. He's had a long stretch of away games, so he's been on the road nonstop since Thanksgiving has passed.

I've slept over at his place a few times, not only because it makes me feel close to Remy, but also because it makes it easier to take care of Krypto. Which just means that I'm able to get unlimited snuggles from our cat.

I don't really find it weird that I've started thinking of Krypto as our cat, even though plenty of others might. I really see a long future with Remy, Thanksgiving just cemented that, so that also means a future with Krypto. Though I've loved the cat since I first met him, hell probably even first heard about him.

I set my water bottle on the counter and get a scoop of food out for the little gremlin and start making some lunch for myself.

I'm coming out of the pantry when I notice a black box set in the wall. I let my curiosity get the best of me and reach out to touch it.

A screen comes to life, and I stand there shocked for a second. I hit the play button and music starts playing through the kitchen.

I look up at the ceiling to find speakers that I've never noticed before. Though to be honest we don't often think to look up.

"What the fuck?" I ask. "Fancy pants McGee over here with his kitchen sound system."

I look over at Krypto and ask, "Did you know about this Toe?"

The little bastard just ignores me and continues to eat his food.

I wave him off as I navigate to Spotify. I don't even think before I put on *The Outsiders Musical* soundtrack and start making some lunch, as I start singing and vibe to the music.

It doesn't take long for my ground beef to brown, and I'm putting the taco seasoning in when "Justice for Tulsa" comes on. I'm not going to lie, even though I love all of the songs on this album, I truly think this is top three of my favorites.

Call me weird but I think my toxic trait is trying to perform literally all the parts in a song. "Bohemian Rhapsody"? Yeah, I'm even singing the guitar parts. It's really no different with "Justice for Tulsa," because I go from signing Cherry's part right into singing Paul's part as if that's a completely normal thing. I'm a one woman cast when it comes to stuff like this.

I'm so in my own world that I don't notice strong arms around my waist and a face burying in the crook of my neck. It only takes me a few seconds to register that there is someone else in the kitchen with me, so I do the only logical thing anyone would, I throw my elbow back as hard as I can and scream. My assailant goes down and I turn around wielding the spatula to see Remy doubled over.

CHAPTER 49
REMINGTON

When I walk into my apartment after this last stretch of road games, I'm immediately hit with two things: the smell of tacos and the sound of Eliza singing every part of a song having to do with Tulsa, though I'm not familiar with it.

I round the corner and lean up against the wall as I watch. My beautiful girlfriend has her back to me at the stove and is dancing slightly. I realize that she found the sound system, and smile to myself. I love that she's comfortable enough in my apartment to do stuff like this.

I set my bag on the ground and take three big steps to cover the distance to Eliza. Without even thinking about it, I wrap my arms around her waist and bury my face in her neck. In the same instance she throws one of her elbows into my stomach hard, and screams.

I double over as Eliza turns around wielding a spatula.

The second she sees and registers that it's me she put the spatula on the counter and grabs my face.

"Oh my god!" Eliza exclaims. "Nash, I'm so sorry. I thought you were a fucking intruder."

I smile through the pain and reply, "Good to know you can hold your own, babe."

Eliza pulls my head to her chest, and I instinctively wrap my arms around her waist, taking in her scent. She smells and feels like *home*.

"I didn't know you were coming home today," she says.

"We got in like an hour ago and I could only think of getting home to you."

I close my eyes as Eliza runs her fingers through my hair. I love it when she does that.

After a few minutes I tell her, "I got you something."

She pulls back and says, "Your birthday is in a few days, why the hell did you get *me* something?"

I give her a quick kiss and reply, "I like spoiling my girl."

Eliza shakes her head.

I pull out a small jewelry box and hand it to her. I watch as her eyes go wide as she tentatively takes the box from me.

"Shit," I say. "It's not a ring."

"Oh, thank fuck," Eliza visibly relaxes. "I love you, but I don't want to move *that* fast."

"Even though nothing about our relationship has exactly been slow?" I ask.

"Yeah," she replies.

I trail my hand down her arm and tell her, "I don't plan on proposing for a while."

"We haven't even had the marriage talk," she replies.

I tuck one of her curls behind her ear and say, "I know, but I think we're on the same page about it."

Eliza doesn't hesitate. "We are."

"Good. Then this isn't a not happening thing, it's a not right now thing."

She nods and smiles at me.

"Okay seriously though, open it," I encourage.

Eliza slowly lifts the top of the box, still staring at me before she looks down. Her mouth drops open slightly as she carefully pulls out the small necklace with the number 26 on it.

"Nash," she breathes, looking up at me.

I explain, "I know you've said a few times that Zeke believes that twenty-six is y'all's lucky number, it also happens to hold significance for you when it comes to hockey. Ramirez getting his first shutout at your first game and then it being my number.

"But it's also significant to the two of us. Not only is it my number, but we first locked eyes with each other on October 26th. This way you're able to always have your lucky number with you."

Eliza doesn't say anything for a minute, and I start to think that I might've over stepped. But then she throws her arms around me and kiss the shit out of me.

I lift her up and set her on the countertop as I step between her legs.

When she pulls away, she says, "It's so fucking thoughtful and that's so fucking beautiful Nash."

I smile at her and reply, "I love you so fucking much Eliza Grace."

Eliza stokes my cheek and says, "I love you like the moon loves the stars."

I smile. "To the moon and back."

"Infinity and beyond."

I let out a small laugh at her reference, but it genuinely fits us.

"Now help me get this on," Eliza says excitedly. "I'm never gonna take it off."

I gently take the necklace from her and move her hair out of the way. I get it clasped and let my hands linger on Eliza's shoulders.

She pulls me forward by a fistful of my shirt and wraps her legs around my waist.

"Now fuck me while I have nothing but this necklace on," she demands.

"Yes ma'am," I reply picking her up and taking her to the couch to do exactly that. I plan on making her wish come true many, many times.

CHAPTER 50
ELIZA

'm lying in bed with Remy when my phone starts ringing, and I immediately recognize Athena's ringtone.

"Hey Thena," I answer. "What's up?"

The second she starts talking I hear how panicked she is, and I sit up. I know Athena and she is not one that easily panics over things, that's more of Cam's style.

"It's all a mess, Lizzie," she practically wails.

"Woah," I say. "Take a deep breath and tell me what's a mess."

On the other end I hear Athena take a couple of deep breaths as Remy wraps a hand around my thigh and looks up at me with concern.

Finally, she tells me, "It's supposed to be day one of post, but my editor just up and quit."

"Do you know why?" I ask.

Athena sniffles, which is how I really know that this has her all out of sorts. Athena Parker is not one to randomly cry over things, something has to really get under her skin to make her cry.

"No," she says. "He just said he couldn't work with me."

"Blacklist him then," I tell her, dead serious.

That's one thing about the film industry, if you aren't doing your job like you're supposed to then people aren't afraid to tell others, especially if it's a common occurrence. If you get talked about in a bad way enough, your chances of someone wanting to work with you exponentially decrease.

"In fact," I tell her. "Give me his name and I'll do it. It is my field after all."

"But what if it's a legitimate reason?" Athena asks.

I love her, but she always wants to see the good in people. Which isn't usually a bad thing, just in this instance it makes things slightly more difficult.

"Thena," I start. "If there was a legit reason as to why he couldn't work for you, he would have told you."

She sighs.

I continue as Remy stokes up and down my thigh, letting me know he's there for me, "Do you really want someone on your team that doesn't have basic communication skills?"

"No," she replies, sounding slightly better.

"Exactly."

I run my fingers through Remy's hair as Athena asks, "Would you be willing to be my editor? You were my first choice, but you know the schedules didn't line up."

I put her on speaker and quickly look at my calendar. I have to let Quincy know if I'm going to go to Scotland for filming soon. I had already told him that I wasn't going to edit the dallies on set.

If I do end up going that means that I'd be leaving sometime between March and April at the earliest. It might be stretching myself a little, but I'm willing to make it work for Athena.

"Yeah, I can do that," I tell her.

She almost squeals and says, "Liz you are literally the best. We'll talk details when you get here."

"Just send me the address and I'll be there in twenty," I reply.

With that she hangs up and I turn to Remy.

"Everything okay?" he asks.

I scoot down the bed until I'm back to lying next to him and reply, "Athena's editor just randomly quit on her with no explanation."

He wraps an arm around my waist and says, "Shit, that's awful."

"Yeah."

"That's why you want to blacklist him?"

"Who knows if he's done something like this before? In our line of work, we need to know the people we're working with are reliable."

His fingers slip under the bottom of my shirt.

"That's understandable," he says. "It's like with hockey and how you have to have a trust in your teammates to do what they're supposed to."

I nod. "Yeah. I feel bad because I *was* her first choice, it's just that the schedules didn't line up. It's kinda giving a Micheal J. Fox vibe with *Back to the Future*."

He gives me a questioning look and asks, "What do you mean by that?"

I run my fingers over his jawline and answer, "When they were casting for *Back to the Future*, they originally wanted Micheal J. Fox as Marty, but because he was doing *Family Ties* it wasn't going to work out. So, they casted Eric Stoltz and got through about six weeks of filming before they fired him. They were able to work something out with Micheal J. Fox, obviously."

Remy smiles up at me and replies, "I love how your brain works."

I smile at him before bringing his lips to mine.

He breaks the kiss and asks, "So you're her editor now?"

I love this man, so fucking much.

"Yes," I reply. "I've never had this many projects so close together though."

Remy kisses my shoulder and says, "I believe you'll be fine."

I smile at his faith in me. It's not like I'll be working on these projects at the same time. I think that's going to be my only saving grace in this.

"That means I have to get out of bed first," I tell him.

Remy dramatically groans and says, "But I feel like I just got home."

I kiss his cheek and reply, "Well now I have to go to work."

He pinches my side and says, "Fine, but you're making it up to me later, sexy lady."

I kiss his lips and reply, "Deal. Now rest up for when I get home, because I'm going to run you for your money and have my way with you."

"Yes ma'am."

I get up to get dressed and as I'm walking away from the bed Remy slaps my ass.

I shake my head and say, "Don't tempt me, Nashville."

"If anyone tempts anyone, it's you babe," he calls out as I walk into the closet. "My little temptress."

I come out, kiss him, and reply, "You're very own siren."

His hands go to my hips as he tries to pull me closer.

"I think temptress sounds better."

I smile. "Better than harlot."

Remy barks out a laugh. "You're anything but a harlot, darling."

"I'm leaving now," I tell him. "So, behave."

"Whatever you say darling."

With that I grab my keys and head out the door.

When I put my car in park, I quickly kill the engine and rush into the postproduction suite. I blame Remy for almost making me late.

When Athena sees me, she immediately gets up and throws her arms around me.

"Oh my god," she says. "You're such a life saver babes. Like seriously, you have no idea."

We sit down and start talking business. Athena goes over the timeline with me, and the potential days we'll need for other stuff that is relevant to my job.

"Any questions or concerns," Athena asks me once she's done.

"I'm potentially going to Scotland when Quincy's film starts shooting," I say.

"Ooh, that's interesting," she replies.

I let out a laugh. "He wanted me to edit dailies on set, but I told him that's not my style and I didn't want to. But he still offered to fly me out during shooting."

"That's fucking awesome Liz!"

I lean back in the chair. "I know right."

"Does Remy know?"

I sigh. "No."

Athena smacks my arm and exclaims, "Eliza Grace!"

"What? I haven't decided yet, so I don't really want to tell him unless I know for sure."

Athena levels a look at me, and I shrink back a little. She's always done this and it's freaky as fuck.

"You need to tell him," she says. "Even if you are only just thinking about it."

I sigh again. "I know, I know."

After a minute I say, "If we haven't locked before I would likely have to leave, I'd need to take the project with me."

Athena waves me off, "That's no problem. I trust you to get it done no matter where you are. You're like my Gayln Susman with *Toy Story 2*."

I smile and turn towards the computer. I make a mental note to bring my hard drive tomorrow so I can have a backup of a backup.

"Is the footage labeled and organized?" I ask.

"If my DIT or assistant editor did their jobs. You'll meet your second tomorrow."

A DIT is a digital imagine technician, and they basically bridge the gap from production to post. So I hope to god that they did their job, because as cathartic as it is to label audio and footage, I'd rather not have to waste time on it.

"Awesome," I reply. "Let's start editing a movie, shall we?"

Athena rubs her hands together and excitedly says, "Yes! I can't wait for you to work your magic on this one. I'm possibly even more excited for this one than *Down Comes Night,* but she'll always be my baby."

I smile and get to work.

CHAPTER 51
REMINGTON

Christmas comes and goes, so does New Years and now we're nearing Valentine's day. It's crazy how fast time is flying.

When Eliza took that editing job for Athena it was hard on us for a while, especially since it was the first time she's really been working on a project while we've been together, but we eventually were able to fall into a routine. We may not get to see each other every day, but that was already our norm.

Currently I'm on a stretch of away games and I haven't seen Eliza in a few days, which it also doesn't help that we've been on a bit of a losing streak these past few games. Luckily time zones don't always bother her, since she's usually up late at home anyways whether working or doing something else.

This is the first time that I've seen her in working mode, even though I haven't actually seen what she does I still think it's very impressive. I also think it's hot as hell, but I always think anything Eliza does is hot.

Every version of Eliza makes me that much more attracted to her and makes me fall even more in love with her.

I'm currently sitting on the plane waiting for the rest of the team to get on when I get a text notification from Eliza.

I click on it to find a picture of myself as I was walking the tarmac to get onto the plane. It must be one that the social team took to post. In the picture I have my carryon suitcase and am dressed in my suit with a backwards cap on. I also notice that my two-day old beard is really noticeable.

THE FUTURE MRS. MILLER

This guy is so fucking hot. I'm totally making this pic my home screen wallpaper

I smile.

ME

Not your lockscreen?

THE FUTURE MRS. MILLER

That is reserved for a certain crop top pic. This one is just for my eyes.

My smile widens.

ME

Little backwards don't you think

THE FUTURE MRS. MILLER

Nope not at all

ME

Is this what does it for you?

THE FUTURE MRS. MILLER

The scruff. *Chef's kiss* The backwards hat. *Chef's kiss* The hair poking out from under the hat. *Chef's kiss*

ME

Really??

THE FUTURE MRS. MILLER

I'm not done

The suit. *Chef's kiss* That ass? 😵. The man. *Chef's fucking kiss*

My smile widens even more. If she makes me smile anymore, I'm afraid my face will break.

ME

That all?

THE FUTURE MRS. MILLER

For now. You are really rocking that look baby. Too bad I don't get to experience it in person

Also you should def wear more backwards hats around me

ME

Just wait until playoff season when I won't be shaving

THE FUTURE MRS. MILLER

Don't jinx us. Knock on wood or Jake's head if he's near. We don't need any bad juju

ME

The way we're playing, minus these past few games, I know we can make it

THE FUTURE MRS. MILLER

I know you don't know Atlanta sports like I do so just trust me. We don't need to be jinxed. You know how hockey players are "superstitious"??

ME

Yes

I have no idea where Eliza is going with this but I'm willing to entertain her.

THE FUTURE MRS. MILLER

In my humble opinion the fans are so much
worse

ME

THE FUTURE MRS. MILLER

Yeah I know. It's not like what we do really has
any impact or anything. We just like to think
it does

ME

I don't think fans are that superstitious

I know what she's told me in the past, but I'm still skeptical about the fans being just as superstitious as us players.

THE FUTURE MRS. MILLER

Trust me they are

Just like y'all have your pregame rituals, the
fans have their game day rituals

ME

I'll take your word for it babe.

THE FUTURE MRS. MILLER

I'm just saying we might be at the same game
but we experience different aspects of it.

She's right. I only see myself play when watching tapes, but that's to see what needs improving. I also don't experience the crowd from the stands, only from the ice. It's interesting to me the kind of perspective Eliza has on the game versus what my perspective of it is.

Eliza sends me a picture of Krypto laying on her chest as she lounges on our couch. I'm not sure when I started thinking of it as *ours,* but it's her space just as much as it is mine, even though she does have her own apartment.

ME

You can't tease me like that

THE FUTURE MRS. MILLER

If I wanted to tease you I'd send you a picture of my boobs

Or my bare pussy spread out on your bed.

I let out a small groan.

ME

You're going to be the death of me woman

THE FUTURE MRS. MILLER

Here lies Nash. Killed by not being able to come in his woman.

Honestly sounds like a shitty way to go

I let out a small laugh.

"Eliza?" Jake asks as he walks by.

"Yep," I reply. "She's being her usual self."

He sits behind me and says, "So torturing you into having blue balls. Tell her I said hi."

I lower the brightness on my phone to help prevent him from seeing anything over my shoulder. It probably wouldn't be a bad idea to invest in one of those privacy screen protector things.

ME

Smitty says hi

THE FUTURE MRS. MILLER

Tell Jake I said hi back

I turn over my shoulder and tell him, "Liza says hi."

"Sweet," he fist pumps the air. "Made my whole night."

ME

The bastard said that made his whole night.

THE FUTURE MRS. MILLER

Shakes head he needs a steady gf. No more hookups

ME

Agreed

I miss you. And Krypto

THE FUTURE MRS. MILLER

We miss you too Nash.

Before Eliza I didn't mind not being at home a lot, though I would worry about Krypto. But since I've met Eliza and gotten to know her on many different levels, the more I'm away the more I just want to be home.

THE FUTURE MRS. MILLER

I love you like the moon loves the stars

I smile.

ME

I love you to the moon and back

THE FUTURE MRS. MILLER

To infinity and beyond

Since my last big stretch of away games that's become our thing. When everything feels so big and out of control, it's a great reminder that I have a woman that loves me, and I love her. I can't wait to one day spend the rest of my life with this woman.

THE FUTURE MRS. MILLER

Go win some hockey games. No one likes a
losing streak

I let out a small laugh and prepare for take off.

CHAPTER 52
ELIZA

'm not surprised when I get a call from Quincy that night. I'm laid out on Remy's couch with Krypto snuggled up on my chest and Remy's game on the tv.

I turn the volume down on the tv before answering.

"Hello," I say.

"Hey Liza," Quincy replies. "You got a minute?"

"Yeah," I answer.

"Good. I guess you have a feeling of where this is going to go?"

I rub Krypto's head and reply, "Your upcoming film. Scotland. If I'm going."

"Bingo," he says, and I can picture him doing finger guns at me. "So, what have you decided?"

I let out a small sigh and reply, "So I'm currently in post for Athena's newest project."

"I didn't realize you had taken on another job."

"It wasn't planned. Her editor quit on day one of post. I was kind of her last option."

"Okay," Quincy says.

"That being said, I'd still like to be flown out during shooting, but I won't be able to be there for the entirety."

I take a deep breath.

I continue, "I've already cleared this with Athena, but if we haven't locked picture before flying out, then I'll need to bring it with me."

Quincy is usually very understanding, so I'm hoping that he'll be understanding with this.

"That's totally fine," he says.

My shoulders sag in relief.

"We can set it up to where you fly out during the last month of filming around May," he tells me. "That way you have enough time to hopefully lock picture."

"Oh my god. Thank you so much," I reply.

Quincy lets out a laugh. "Liz, you know a lot of us are very understanding when you communicate."

I run a hand through my hair and reply, "Yeah, I know. It's just always nerve wracking having these negotiation conversations."

"Yeah, tell me about it. Well, I gotta go," he says. "I'll have Patty send over all the information."

"Awesome," I reply. "Have a good rest of your night Quin."

"You too Liz. Bye."

"Bye."

I hang up the phone and look at Krypto.

"Guess what Toe," I say. "I'm going to Scotland."

I turn the volume back up on the tv. As much as I love hockey, I would rather be in the arena watching. There's just a different kind of energy when you're watching the game with thousands of other fans, plus it makes the game even more enjoyable.

I text Athena and Cam

SUPER GRAPHIC ULTRA MODERN GIRLS

ME

Guess who's going to Scotland bitches

ATHENA GODDESS OF WISDOM

You actually pulled the trigger?

ME

Yep

CAMILA THE NOLAN WANNABE

Holy fucking shit Liz! That's amazing!!

ATHENA GODDESS OF WISDOM

You told Remy yet?

I glance away from my phone, because no I haven't told him. If I'm being honest, I haven't brought it up since that first time Quincy called about this whole thing.

Shit. May is smack in the middle of playoff season. Like round two into the conference championship.

That is if the Flames make it to the playoffs and can progress that far. But seeing the way they are playing this year; they have a high likelihood of making it.

Even if they do make it, there's no guarantee that they can make it to the Stanley cup finals. Fuck. I can't be thinking like this, especially since I know how Atlanta teams are notorious for chocking when it matters.

CAMILA THE NOLAN WANNABE

I'm taking her silence as a no

ATHENA GODDESS OF WISDOM

What the fuck Liz? You were supposed to talk to him about this like months ago

ME

I know. But it was just a possibility then, not reality.

CAMILA THE NOLAN WANNABE

Babes. You know you still should've talked to him about it. He is your boyfriend after all

ATHENA GODDESS OF WISDOM

Don't say I didn't tell you so when you unintentionally break your man's heart

ME

I'm not going to break his heart

CAMILA THE NOLAN WANNABE

Just don't put it off anymore. And just tell him the truth

ATHENA GODDESS OF WISDOM

Remy loves you so that's all you need to do and he'll understand

I know that they're both right, I do, but fuck I hate this. I'm just afraid something will go wrong.

I don't even want to think about the Flames making the play-offs right now, or really even telling Remy about this stupid trip.

Why did I say yes? Our relationship is still so new.

I snap a picture of the tv and then one of me and Krypto before sending them to Remy.

ME

I know that you likely won't see this till the end of the game but I love you and we're both cheering you on from this huge ass couch

We should get toe a jersey so he can match us

I rest my phone on my chest and take a deep breath. I turn my attention back in hopes that it will take my mind off of this, but it doesn't.

Realistically I know I just need to talk to Remy, but I can't for the life of me figure out why I'm struggling so much with this.

I should just rip the band aid off but I just can't.

What if this hurts your relationship with Nash? A voice says in my head, and there it is. The reason I'm scared out of my fucking mind to tell Remy.

CHAPTER 53
REMINGTON

The Atlanta Flames are heading to the playoffs! I knew we could do it; I just hope that we can stay strong.

All I want to do right now is get home and celebrate this with my girlfriend.

My body aches from some of the brutal hits I took in tonight's game, but that's not going to deter me.

When I walk through my front door, the first thing I notice is the low lighting throughout. The second thing I notice is that Eliza is not in the living room, which is where I'd normally find her.

I set my bag down and call out, "Eliza?"

She doesn't immediately respond to me, which is kind of weird. Though she has been acting a little strange the past few weeks, but I've just chalked it up to her job.

I'm about to call our for her again when she walks out of my room in my jersey, nothing but my jersey.

She smiles sweetly at me and says, "Hey hot stuff."

I bite my knuckles and reply, "Fuck Eliza. You are like a goddess."

My eyes trail up her long, toned legs as she walks toward me.

I can't help but wonder what she has on beneath my jersey; I hope she has on nothing.

"I'm gonna need you to strip to your boxers and get on the couch," Eliza more demands than tells me.

She doesn't have to tell me twice.

"Yes ma'am," I reply as I start to pull off my shirt as I walk to the couch.

I quickly drop my pants and sit on the couch. Eliza takes no time to push me back and straddle my lap.

There's no hiding how turned on I am right now.

Eliza slowly lowers herself over my erection, and as soon as she is fully seated on my lap I can feel how wet she is. I just wish there were no barriers between us.

"You're already so wet for me, baby," I tell her.

Eliza moves her hips and lets out a moan.

I trail my hands up the outside of her thighs and slowly bunch my jersey up at her hips, only to be met with her bare pussy.

If it was possible to get any harder than I already am, then I definitely would get harder.

I run my thumb over her center and say, "Fuck baby. You didn't tell me I'd be getting to see your bare pussy when I lifted my jersey."

Eliza wastes no time in grabbing the back of my head and slamming her lips to mine.

My hands run up her thighs and squeeze, causing Eliza to move her hips again and I thrust up into her. She bites my bottom lip causing me to groan and thrust up again.

I pull away and say, "Sweetheart, if I don't get inside of you right now, I'm going to combust."

She gives me a mischievous smile and wags her finger at me as she replies, "Uh uh. Nope."

I let out a whine but Eliza cups me through my boxers, and I thrust into her hand.

I think that she's going to fully remove her hand from my

dick, but instead she lifts up her hips and moves for the waist-band of my boxers.

I quickly lift my hips a little so she can easily pull my boxers down.

My cock springs free and Eliza gives me a couple of quick pumps.

With my hands still on her hips I try to bring her down, but she doesn't budge. Eliza just moves her other hand under my jersey.

I lift it up and watch her circle her clit a couple of times before running a finger through her wetness. When she gets to her entrance, she thrusts one finger in and pumps a couple of times before adding a second.

I go to touch myself and Eliza slaps my hand away before squeezing my balls.

My hips instinctively jolt forward as I exclaim, "Fuck! Eliza I'm not going to last much longer."

She just smiles as me and releases her grip on my balls and removes her fingers from her wet pussy.

Eliza presses her fingers against my mouth and says, "Open."

I open and bring them into my mouth. I can taste her arousal on them as I swirl her fingers in my mouth.

"Suck, pretty boy," she commands.

She doesn't need to tell me twice, and once she's satisfied Eliza removes her fingers from my mouth with a pop.

Eliza leans in and whispers before kissing me, "Let's get to the main event, shall we?"

Without breaking the kiss Eliza reaches between us and grips my cock as she aligns it with her entrance, before fully seating herself to my hilt.

"Oh fuck," I moan. "You feel so fucking good, baby."

Her hands got to my hair, and she says, "Touch me."

"What's the magic word, Eliza Grace?"

Eliza tries to move her hips, only for me to stop her and she lets out a frustrated groan.

I lock eyes with her, and we just sit there for a minute. Man, I fucking love her.

Eliza huffs and says, "Fine. Will you *please* touch me?"

I give her a devilish grin as I reply, "I thought that you'd never ask darlin."

She slaps my shoulder and stutters as I circle her clit, "A-ass."

I don't get to reply because Eliza lifts herself up and slams back down, causing us both to groan.

"Nash," Eliza cries. "I'm so close."

"Fuck baby, we've barley gotten started."

I flick her clit and meet her hips with mine as she slams back down.

"I only wish I could see your beautiful tits bouncing as you impale yourself on my dick."

She shakes her head and says, "Jersey stays on."

Something possessive in me growls as I flip us over. Eliza immediately wraps her legs around my waist and deepens the angle.

She pulls my head to hers and I kiss her jaw making my way up to her mouth.

I feel her tighten around me and on my next thrust she's screaming, "Nash!"

Hearing Eliza call out my name always gets me closer.

I roughly thrust into her a couple more times before I feel my release as my come fills her up.

I collapse on Eliza, careful not to crush her.

We both breath heavy as I carefully pull out, and we both groan at the loss of contact. I look down to find my come running down her leg.

I scoop it up with my finger and say, "Open."

She does and I stick my fingers in her mouth. Immediately Eliza's tongue circles the tips of my fingers. I pull them out and cup her face before leaning in to kiss her.

The taste of me on Eliza's lips is almost enough to get me hard again, but my body is already worn out for the night.

I roll off of Eliza and corner her in the crease of the couch.

"I've never fucked someone in my jersey," I say and move a rouge curl behind her ear.

Eliza lightly wraps her arms around my neck and replies, "Good. I'll be the only one you fuck in your jersey."

I smile and she continues, "I've never been fucked while wearing someone's jersey, but it's always been on my list of things to do."

I nip at her bottom lip and say, "Next time I'm going to fuck you from behind so I can see my last name sprawled across your back."

"Mmh," she replies sleepily. "Can't wait, Nashy."

I grab the blanket off the back of the couch and throw it over us before pulling up my boxers. I wrap my arm around Eliza, and she snuggles up against me.

I kiss her temple and whisper, "Good night, Eliza Grace. I love you."

With her eyes closed she says, "I love you too Nash."

It's not long after that Eliza is asleep. I'm not far behind her, and even though I might regret sleeping on the couch in the morning, I don't care right now.

CHAPTER 54
ELIZA

Picture lock is supposed to be today. I haven't told anyone because it's not always guaranteed that we do lock the picture on the day we're supposed to, and I really don't want to jinx it.

The only problem is my brain thinks it can start worrying about telling Remy about Scotland. Because, no, I still haven't told him yet. That would've been the logical thing, and my brain hasn't been very logical about this whole situation I've gotten myself into.

The worrying is getting to me enough that I can't really keep anything down, and I'm not a worry puker; I don't puke much in general. It's bad enough that I have to stop at Zeke's to expel this mess, because I refuse to puke on the side of the road in the middle of Atlanta.

I'm barely holding it together when Zeke opens the door, because of course this is the one time I don't have my keys on my person.

"Why did you knock?" he asks, shutting the door behind me.

I swallow and reply, "Don't have my keys."

I don't stop until I'm in his bathroom and on my knees. I get the toilet lid open just before throwing up.

Once it's out I sit there with my hair pulled back and my head in the toilet bowl for a minute.

"What, are you pregnant or something?" Zeke asks because of fucking course he followed me and that's the first thing that comes to his fucking mind.

I sit back and reply, "No."

"Then what the hell is wrong with you?"

I sigh and reply, "Stress."

I should know better than just giving Zeke one-word answers, because I know he'll pull it out of me eventually. But this whole thing has my body all messed up.

He sits on the floor next to me and asks, "What are you stressing out about that it's bringing you to puke? Because that's not like you."

I turn to lean against the wall, tilting my head back.

"I'm going to Scotland in about a week for filming," I say. "And I haven't told Remy."

Zeke whips his head towards me and exclaims, "You didn't tell me either! You can't just abandon me."

I realize that I have hurt Zeke's feelings by not telling him—and probably hit the nerve with his mommy issues as well—but I can't worry about that right now. Once I sort through my feelings, I'll make it up to him.

"I know, I'm sorry, and I'm not abandoning you," I say. "But I don't have to worry about what impact this could have on my relationship with you."

"And you do with Remy?" Zeke asks.

I can feel the tears threatening to fall.

"Logically I know that there's nothing to worry about, as long as I can actually have this conversation with him."

"How long have you known you were going to do this?"

I look at my brother and reply, "It was only a possibility about end of October, early November, but became a reality a couple of months ago."

"Eliza Grace Fox!" Zeke exclaims.

My hands go to my face, and I say, "I know, I know. It's bad. I just got busy with Athena's newest film and nothing else has really crossed my mind."

Zeke sighs and wraps an arm around my shoulders.

"You need to talk to him. Today," he tells me.

"I know," I reply. "I'm just scared."

"There's literally no reason to be scared, Liz. It's all up here." Zeke taps my temple.

"I know."

"For once baby sister, think with your heart rather than your head." I can still hear the hurt in his voice, and that makes the pit in my stomach drop lower.

"Has anyone ever told you you're a decent big brother when you want to be?" I ask teasing him a little.

"A few times," he replies smugly. "But honestly not enough."

I roll my eyes and jab my elbow into his side.

Zeke stand up and offers me a hand and I take it.

"Now go tell your boyfriend that you're leaving for Scotland in a few days," he says. "For—?"

I whisper, "A month."

"A fucking month!" he yells. "No wonder you're fucking stressing about telling him, but you still have to tell him now."

I reply, "Work first. Gotta picture lock this bitch."

Zeke smiles and walks me to the front door.

"I'm texting Remy tomorrow to see if you've told him," Zeke tells me. "And if you haven't then I feel it's only right you have to deal with the collateral."

I roll my eyes, but I know he's not bluffing. I one hundred percent know that Zeke will text Remy about this tomorrow whether I've told him or not.

"Bye dickhead," I tell him and start to walk away.

"Bye pee breath," he calls after me, and I flip him off.

I just have to get through the rest of today and everything

will be fine. As long as I don't think about the impact this could have on my relationship with Remy, and the fact that I've really hurt Zeke by not telling him.

CHAPTER 55
ELIZA

I fully prepared to tell Remy about Scotland when I got home. I really did. But by the time I got home it took everything in me to kick off my shoes. I face planted on my bed and told myself not to fall asleep.

I have to wait for Nash to get home, I thought as I got in bed.

Remy was out at a team dinner before the playoffs started, so I know that he would be home on the later side. My plan was to talk to him when he got home.

One minute I'm lying face first on my bed, the next I'm practically dead to the world.

When I wake up in the morning I'm tucked under the covers and Remy is sitting next to me, lightly stroking my head.

He feels me stirring and leans down to kiss the top of my head.

"Morning, beautiful," he says.

I rub the sleep out of my eyes and wrap my arms around his waist.

Groggily I ask, "What time did you get home last night?"

Remy runs a hand down my hair in an attempt to smooth it out and replies, "Around two. You were passed out."

"We picture locked yesterday, and I was practically dead on my feet by the time I got home."

Remy looks at me and says, "Why didn't you tell me? That's awesome!"

I shrug and reply, "I never like jinxing it, so I don't usually tell anyone until after."

"Makes sense," he says. "You hungry?"

I nod.

Remy kisses me and tells me, "I'm gonna go make some breakfast."

I roll off him and watch him walk towards the kitchen.

I stretch and move to get out of bed. I'm still wearing what I had on yesterday, so I scoop up one of Remy's shirts and a pair of shorts.

I use the bathroom and head towards Remy, taking a seat at the kitchen island.

"Why is Zeke texting me asking if you've told me about Scotland yet?" Remy asks.

"Shit," I reply.

Of course, my fucking brother can't even wait until the end of the day like a normal person.

"Eliza?" Remy asks curiously.

I run a hand over my face and say, "Do you remember when I was telling you about the director that wanted me to pull a *Baby Driver?*"

He sets a plate in front of me before saying, "Yeah. You pretty much said that you like being able to sit down with all the footage to edit."

I nod and reply, "Yeah. I can't remember if I told you or not but Quincy, the director, wants to fly me out to Scotland for filming, even though I'm not going to be editing the dailies."

Remy stabs his eggs with his fork and replies, "That's awesome, babe! When would you leave?"

I take a deep breath and say, "Friday."

His fork clatters to his plate and I can't bring myself to look up at Remy for a few seconds.

When I work up the courage to meet his eyes, and I can feel tears starting to prick my eyes.

Remy immediately wraps me up in a hug and asks, "Hey, what's wrong baby?"

"I feel so shitty," I cry.

He's so gentle with me as he rubs my back, which only makes me cry harder, and he asks, "Why?"

I can't lie to him; I've never been able to do that, and I don't fucking want to.

"I've known about this for months," I cry, and tell him the whole truth.

Remy pulls back and makes me meet his gaze.

"Why didn't you just talk to me?"

I wipe my nose.

I shrug and answer, "I don't know. At first it was just a possibility, then it became reality, and I was scared about how it'd impact our relationship. I'm still fucking scared about that, because I don't want to ruin what we have."

I take a deep breath and continue, "Then I got busy working on Athena's film and didn't have much brain power to think about it. And you probably think I'm awful for keeping this from you."

Remy cups the sides of my face as I let out a sob and he says, "Hey, hey. It's okay. I don't think you're awful. I understand."

That makes me cry harder. What did I do to ever deserve this man? He knows my soul like it's his own.

Remy pulls me against his chest, and I clutch at him.

"Do you think we'll survive the distance for a month?" I hiccup.

He replies, "I mean we've pretty much already been doing the distance thing, in a way."

I pull back and before I can think about it the words are out of my mouth. "If you don't want to wait for me, I won't hold it against you. Even if it fucking shatters my heart."

Remy's grip on my arms tightens and I watch as his nostrils flare.

"Stop," he commands. "A little distance won't bother me when I know I want to spend an eternity with you."

I hear the words, but they don't really register. My brain is just stuck in panic mode right now.

"It's really okay if you can't wait for me," I say, breaking my heart in the process.

What the fuck is wrong with me? Why the hell am I trying to throw away this really fucking good thing?

Remy takes a deep breath and replies, "The sun could go out and I would still wait an eternity for you. A little distance is nothing when I *know* you are my forever, Eliza Grace. Nothing in this world could stop me from coming to you if given the opportunity."

I can feel the tears running down my face again. Remy quickly wipes them up with his thumb and tilts my chin up.

He continues, "I want to spend eternity with you, and nothing will change that."

The words finally register in my head, and I launch myself at him. I throw my arms around his neck and Remy catches me; he always catches me.

"I love you like the moon loves the fucking stars," I say into his neck.

His grip on me tightens and he replies, "I love you to the fucking moon and back."

"To infinity and beyond," I say.

"To infinity and fucking beyond."

CHAPTER 56
REMINGTON

'm nervous about dropping Eliza off at the airport. Last night we had dinner with Zeke and Jeremiah, so she got to say bye to them last night. She's been waiting to tell me bye, and I already know that I'm going to fucking miss her so much.

I hate that she's not going to be here for playoffs, but I'm not going to stop her from doing what she wants. That would be a real dick move, and that's not who I am.

I pull up to the drop off lane and put the car in park.

Eliza grabs my face and brings my mouth to hers. Her fingers tangle in my hair as my tongue runs across the seam of her lips, seeking entrance.

A car honks nearby, and we reluctantly pull apart.

"I'll text you every day," Eliza says, her lips swollen. "And I'm going to watch your games when I have a chance."

"I'm going to miss you," I reply. "Like so fucking bad."

She smiles and says, "I'm going to miss you too, Nash."

I kiss her again and it doesn't last as long as I would like.

"Okay," she says. "I better go before the people that work at the Hartsfield-Jackson airport start cussing us out."

We both get out and I help get Eliza's suitcase out of the back. When the wheels touch the ground, I wrap her up in my arms.

I'm the first to pull away and Eliza pulls up the handle on her suitcase.

"I love you Nash," she tells me.

"I love you Eliza Grace," I reply.

In a more serious tone she says, "Now go take the Flames to the finals. And don't Atlanta it up."

"What does 'Atlanta it up' mean?" I ask, genuinely not knowing.

Eliza pats my shoulder and answers, "Atlanta teams are notorious for choking in the playoffs, or when it matters."

I trail my finger down her arm and ask, "Can you give me an example?"

"In 2017 the Atlanta Ravens were playing the New England Titans in the Superbowl. We were up twenty-one by half time, then the Titans tied us up sending us into overtime. The titans ended up winning thirty-four to twenty-eight."

It's always so attractive when she talks sports to me.

Eliza continues, "The Ravens stopped playing after halftime, costing us the Superbowl."

"You're so hot when you talk sports to me" I tell her.

A car honks and Eliza says, "I really should go."

I nod and she starts toward the door.

She stops and calls out, "Seriously don't Atlanta it up!"

I smile and reply, "I'll try not to!"

She turns and walks through the door.

I get in my car and pull away from the drop off lane, leaving my heart with the woman that's on her way to Scotland.

For the next month I'll just have to deal with only seeing Eliza through FaceTime calls and Instagram posts. I only wish that she had told me sooner, so we could've spent even more time together before she went off.

CHAPTER 57
REMINGTON

"I haven't seen Eliza yet," Jake comments as he skates over to me during warmups. "Is she going to be here tonight?"

"Are you trying to hit on my girl?" I ask teasing him.

Grant comes up just as I say that and replies, "Who is Smitty trying to steal now?"

"My girlfriend," I say with a shrug.

Jake opens and closes his mouth a few times before replying, "No I'm not. I was just curious if Eliza was going to be here tonight, because she's kind of my friend."

"Does she know that?" Grant asks, leaning on his stick.

Jake swats him on the chest and says, "You're a dick you know that?"

I hold back a laugh. I swear it's like being with children most of the time. I think Max might be better behaved than this sometimes.

Grant rolls his eyes and turns to me and points out, "Seriously though, I haven't seen her yet. And I know that she's normally here by now."

"Wow," I deadpan. "Nice to know you have my girlfriend's habits memorized."

Grant levels a look at me and replies, "I don't, but I know

from previous seasons that her seat is rarely empty. It's kind of hard not to notice when someone sits in the same spot so close to the ice."

He has me there, and I will admit, it's only been one day and I'm already wigging out.

I let out a sigh, I know it will be better to just rip the bandaid off.

"No," I start. "She won't be here tonight."

Jake gives me a questioning look as he asks, "Is everything all right? You two aren't in a fight or anything are you? Because I really can't be a child of divorce, again."

I let out a sharp laugh and I reply, "I sometimes don't understand you, Smitty."

"Y'all are like the standard. Endgame even, and if I have to chose sides I don't know if I would be able to," he explains.

"Ignore him," Grant says. "Why won't Eliza be joining us?"

I shuffle my skates a couple times, trying to stall the inevitable.

I let out another sigh and explain, "I dropped her off at the airport yesterday."

Jake's jaw drops open and he exclaims, "Aw fuck! I knew! Mom and dad are having problems!"

I reach over and smack him upside the head and give him a hard glare.

"No we aren't," I react. "She just went to Scotland."

"Cap back me up here," Jake says. "But one doesn't *just* go to fucking Scotland."

Grant shrugs slightly and replies, "I have to agree with Smitty on this, Ratatouille. People really don't just leave the country unless there is a reason."

I narrow my eyes at the two of them.

Why did I ever become friends with them? I think before mentally laughing at myself. *Oh my god. That is totally something Liza would say.*

I shake my head as I tell them, "She was invited to be on set for a film that is filming in Scotland, and she decided to take it."

"And how do you feel about this?" Grant, the ever intuitive one asks.

I tilt my head back and stare at the ceiling for a moment before looking back at the ice.

"I'm happy for her, but I also wish that she had told me sooner so we could've really made this time count."

"How long is she gone for?" Jake asks.

"A fucking month," I practically whine.

Their mouths drop open. I don't blame them, that's really about how I felt when Eliza first told me. It truly was a shock to the system when she said those words, though I think it was even more shocking hearing when she would be leaving.

Grant is the first one to recover and asks, "And how are you doing?"

"I'm fucking miserable," I whine. "I know this whole season we've often been like ships passing in the night. But this is a whole new level because I don't even have the reassurance that she'll be at home when I get back."

"Is this why you've been kind of snippy?" Jake asks.

I tilt my head slightly and reply, "Yes. Even Krypto misses her."

Grant grabs me by the shoulder and says, "You know we're here for you."

"Yeah I know."

"I'm not going to come into your bed and cuddle you though," Jake quickly says. "I love you like a brother, but that crosses too many lines for me."

"What the fuck is wrong with you?" I ask jokingly. "I wouldn't want your smelly ass in my bed anyways."

Jake pretends to wipe his brow and exhales, "Whew."

I roll my eyes and say, "I also don't think you would be as soft as Liza is Smitty. I've seen what you look like under all that gear and it doesn't appeal to me."

Jake throws his hand up to his heart and gasps as if he's been hurt. "And here I thought you loved seeing my naked body."

"With that I'm going to go stretch," I say. "Far away from you."

"Love you too man!" Jake yells as I skate away.

I make my way over to the side where Eliza normally sits and see Jeremiah getting up and making his way to the glass. I have a feeling what is about to go down.

I stop in front of him on my side of the glass, and he pulls something out of his pocket. He tosses it over and I easily catch the small bag.

Like that time Eliza was in LA for a film premiere, it's a small bag of Hershey Kisses with a note attached.

I look up at Jeremiah, smile, and mouth to him *Thank you.*

He sharply nods his head and turns back to his seat.

I know that Jeremiah is missing his baby girl just like me. Only he misses her as her father, and I miss her as my girlfriend.

I pull off the note and read it.

Nash,

I already miss you so fucking much. I don't know how I'm going to survive this fucking month, but I will prevail. I'm going to enjoy the fuck out of this trip no matter how much I miss your sexy face.

Anyways, I've prepared for my dad to give you one of these every home game you have during the playoffs (as long as he's there). Now you're probably thinking when did I have the time to do this, and I'll say I have my ways. No I just did this when you were on the road, and when I was taking breaks during editing.

I'll be rooting for the Flames all the way here in Scotland. Hopefully I can catch a few games live, if not I'll just watch the replay. I know that we'll text plenty, but calling and FaceTime are the next best options.

Tell the boys not to Atlanta this up. I would really like to see the Flames make it to the finals.

I love you to the moon and back, Nashville. Infinity and beyond the whole fucking galaxy.

Love,

Your Eliza.

Ps. In case I don't see you: good afternoon, good evening, and goodnight.

I shake my head and laugh at her *Truman Show* reference. I swear, I never get tired of the film references that Eliza seemingly pulls out of nowhere. It's wild to me how she has a quote for just about everything.

Man I fucking love this woman.

I skate back over to the bench and get Zack to take Eliza's gift back to my stall.

I shake out my body, and start preparing my mind to play sixty minutes of hockey, because I too would like to see this team make it to the Stanley Cup finals.

CHAPTER 58
ELIZA
ONE MONTH LATER

For a whole month I've been in Scotland for the filming of Quincy's newest film. I've enjoyed it, really, but I'm ready to get home to see my loved ones. I've only seen Remy and my family through a screen for the past month, and I'm tired of it. I'm a homebody anyways, so it's not all that surprising. Which is why I'm currently hurtling about 600 miles per hour at 30,000 feet in the air in route to Atlanta.

Filming is still going on, but when I told Quincy I was ready to get home, he completely understood. Which I am so thankful for.

Tonight, the Flames play the final game in the semis to see who advances to the Stanley Cup finals. I'm so fucking proud of not just Remy, but also the whole team. This entire playoff run they've fought tooth and nail to get where they are now.

Over the past month I was only ever able to catch Remy's games live a couple of times, mostly the couple of days where we were doing night shoots. But I still watched the replays, and I still cheered Remy and the rest of the Flames on.

Remy doesn't know that I'm coming back today, I want to surprise him. I know he'll be so fucking glad to see me in person, and once again be in the same time zone.

This past month has taken a toll on the both of us, but we've survived. We've talked on the phone as much as possible given our schedules, and the man has liked every single post on Instagram I've posted, but I miss him. If I ever get another invitation to be flown out for filming, I'm making sure it's during the off season so Remy can go with me.

In about nine or so hours I'll be back on Georgia soil, and I'll get to see my boyfriend. I just hope that I'll be able to sleep some on this flight.

The second I see my dad waiting by the baggage claim I run over to him and throw my arms around his neck.

"Daddy!" I exclaim.

"Oh, my baby girl," he hugs me tighter. "I've missed you EG."

"I'm here too," Zeke says.

I'm not going to lie I didn't even know that Zeke was here, or that he was coming. Though I guess I can't really be all that surprised, this is my twin brother we're talking about.

I let go of dad and throw my arms around my brother.

"It's good to have you back, baby sister," he tells me.

I release him and punch him in the arm as I reply, "I'm ten minutes younger."

Zeke just smiles at me, and I can't help but smile back.

My dad smiles and asks, "Do you need help with your bag?"

I look over my shoulder and see my suitcase on the carrousel and go to grab it. Zeke beats me to it though, and easily lifts it.

"What the fuck do you have in this thing?" he asks, pretending like my suitcase is heavier than it is. "Bricks?"

I reply with sarcasm heavy on my words, "Yeah, I put them in there just for you."

He narrows his eyes and opens his mouth to say something,

but dad cuts him off. "Alright you two. Let's not draw more attention to ourselves."

Right cause my brother *is* a famous tight end for the Atlanta Ravens. So even with the hat he has on, he'll still get recognized.

I don't mind it, I grew up with it with Zeke, and now I've gotten more used to it with Remy.

"Right," Zeke says. "We have a girl to get to her boyfriend's hockey game so she can surprise him. Let's roll Cinderella."

I roll my eyes as we start toward the door, and I let my dad and Zeke lead the way to the parked car.

"Do you want to stop by your apartment before the game?" Dad asks me from the driver's seat.

I look at the time.

Nash has likely already left for the arena, I think.

In response I ask, "You have my jersey?"

Dad nods and replies, "Yes ma'am."

I take two seconds to think about it before asking, "Can we stop at Remy's?"

Zeke whips his head back at me and exclaims, "Are you trying to ruin your surprise?"

"He's likely already left for the arena dipshit," I reply.

"But you don't know for sure?" Zeke questions.

I look him dead in the eye and say, "Nash always gets to the arena an hour before the doors open. So that means he has likely already left."

Zeke opens his mouth, but dad asks, "Can you give me directions?"

"Of course."

I make Zeke carry my suitcase up to Remy's apartment and when I step through the door, I see Krypto lounging on the back of the couch.

"So, this is where the famous Remy Miller lives," Zeke comments as he looks around.

I roll my eyes and tell Zeke, "Stay here."

"Why?" he asks.

"Krypto doesn't do well with strangers," I reply and start walking towards the couch. "Toe!"

Krypto looks up at me and chirps as he jumps down. He runs to me and rubs up against my legs before I scoop him up. I bury my face in his fur as he loudly purrs.

"Oh, I missed you Krypto," I say.

I set him down on the floor and turn to find Zeke leaning against the wall with a smirk on his face.

To Krypto I say, "I'll be back later Toe. Okay?" To Zeke I say, "Wipe that smirk off your face, it really doesn't fucking suit you."

"Domestic life suits you sis," he replies opening the door.

"Come on dickface, dad is waiting on us."

When we get to the arena, I'm so jittery it's not funny.

I know that Remy's family is going to be here, I also know that I'm meeting up with them before the game, because that's the plan we came up with.

I've been planning this for the past couple of days and I wouldn't have been able to pull this off if it hadn't been for my dad, Zeke, and Remy's family.

It doesn't take us long to find the Millers when we get inside. I hug everyone in greeting.

"Are you excited?" Georgia asks.

I take a deep breath and reply, "Nervous more than anything."

Max grabs my hand and says, "Don't be nervous Iza."

I smile at him.

The plan is not to be seen by Remy until after the game. I don't want to mess up his routine before this game, and even if me being back is a good thing I know I can still mess with his game.

Tonight, I'm sitting in the suite Remy was able to get for his family, while my dad and Zeke take our normal seats.

My dad will give Remy the final note that I had prewritten, and the Hershey kisses that go with it. If all goes according to plan, at the end of the game Jake and Grant will make sure that Remy stays on the ice until I'm able to get down there.

There are so many moving parts, and so much could go wrong but win or lose, I will be surprising my man tonight. It'll be sweeter if the Flames win, but I'm not going to jinx anything. But in the end, as long as I see Remy nothing else really matters.

"Alright family," I say encompassing not only my blood family, but also my future family. "Let's get this show on the road."

Everyone around me cheers, and we head to our seats to watch this game unfold.

CHAPTER 59
REMINGTON

This whole game we have been fighting tooth and nail against the Florida Oilers. We've pretty much stayed tied up for the first two periods, and that's no different in the third.

I watch the clock counting down and coach puts me and my line on for our last shift of the game.

Misha is able to get the puck and sends it to Grant. I block one of the Oilers players and manage to get open. Grant passes to me and I see an opening.

I shoot the puck by their goalie's left side. He's just not quick enough to stop it as it sails by. The goal lights go off and I'm immediately swarmed by my teammates.

I look up at the scoreboard to see the time and watch the replay. We have ten seconds left on the clock and I'm pretty sure I just scored the game winning goal.

I know the Oilers don't have much fight in them because we don't either, but I hope our team doesn't give up too soon. That won't do well in our favor if we stop playing the game too soon.

When my teammates get off my back I skate over toward our bench. I hop the wall and am met with slaps on the back as I squirt water in my mouth.

The next line gets ready for the face off. Swanson, one of our third line centers, leans down prepared for when the ref drops the puck.

Luckily, we win the face off and my eyes go to the clock.

The buzzer sounds and we all clear the bench. We're going to the fucking Stanley Cup finals.

Holy fucking shit! I scored the game winning goal that is sending us to the fucking finals.

Grant smacks me on the back and says, "Come on Rata-touille, let's get a team picture."

I follow him and Jake, but the only thing I can think about is Eliza not being here to celebrate this with me.

There's confetti flying everywhere and this should be a really happy moment, but all I can fucking think about is missing my girlfriend.

"Hey superstar!" a voice calls out.

I whip around so fast I almost fall on my ass, because I know that voice. I would know that voice anywhere.

Eliza stands there on the ice smiling up at me.

I'm frozen in place for a second before rushing to her and scooping her up. Eliza wraps her legs around my waist, obviously not minding that I likely smell like rotten eggs in a landfill.

She runs her fingers over the beard that I've grown out and says, "You've gotten all scruffy on me."

"What the fuck are you doing here?" I ask still not believing that this is real.

She smiles and replies, "I was ready to be home, and I wanted to surprise you."

I beam up at her and say, "Consider me surprised."

Eliza pulls my face to hers and I kiss her for the first time in a month. I don't even care who's watching, I practically devour my woman's face right there on the ice.

If they want to take pictures of us, I'll frame them and display them in our living room. That's how much I don't care about anything other than Eliza in this moment

Eliza pulls back with a smile on her swollen lips, and I let out a groan.

She lets out a small laugh and exclaims, "You're going to the fucking finals!"

My smile widens now that I'm able to celebrate this with her.

Jake and Grant skate over and Eliza looks to them and says, "Thank you."

They nod and I ask, "What are you thanking them for Eliza Grace?"

Jake responds, "For keeping you on the ice until she got down here. Because we know that you would've tried going back to the locker room so you could sulk."

I stare into Eliza's beautiful blue-gray eyes before asking, "How long have you been here?"

"My flight got in a couple of hours before the game started," she replies.

I pinch her ass, and she lets out a short shriek.

"Smartass," I say.

"Yeah, but I'm your smartass," she replies.

I kiss her again, this time less desperate and slower.

"Okay," Jake interrupts. "Cut it out with the PDA you two. We've got some celebrating to do."

Eliza looks at me and tells me, "You can thank both our families for helping with this surprise."

I reluctantly set her down and ask, "You've been here for the whole game?"

"Of course," she hip checks me and laces her fingers with mine. "I couldn't sit in my normal seat and risk you seeing me. I didn't want to mess with your game."

I turn her to face me and say, "I love you so much."

She smiles and replies, "I love you too Nash."

Oh, how I've missed her saying that.

"Can't I just take you home now?" I ask.

Eliza, the tease that she is, just replies, "Celebrations now, then you can fuck me with your last name sprawled across my back later."

Have I said that the love of my life is going to be the death of me?

"I never realized how attractively dirty Eliza's mouth is," Jake says, as she walks towards our families. I completely forgot that him and Grant were over here.

Grant smacks him upside the head and tells Jake, "Watch it Smitty. That's Ratatouille's woman."

"Damn right," I reply, watching as she walks over to our families. "I'm gonna spend an eternity with her, because I know for a fucking fact I'm gonna marry that woman one day."

EPILOGUE

ELIZA

I look at my dad and ask, "Are you ready for this?"

"Liza," he replies. "This is the first time in five years that the Flames have made it to the finals. Of course I'm fucking ready."

"Yo!" Zeke calls out. "Wait for me."

I roll my eyes, but we stop and wait for Zeke to join us with his mountain of food.

"Yeah, I know dad, but if they win this game—"

"They win the championship," my dad finishes for me.

Max runs up to me and smacks into my legs, trying to hug me.

I scoop him up and ask, "You ready to see Rex play Maxie?"

He throws his hands up in the air and yells, "Go Flames!"

I toss him up and catch him, causing Max to giggle.

"Alright Max Verstappen," I say. "Let's go."

When warmups start, Remy immediately skates over to us. Max can barely contain his excitement. While he doesn't completely understand what's going on, Max understands enough to be excited, plus he gets to see Remy.

As Remy tosses over a puck for Max he mouths to me, *To the moon and back.*

I smile and mouth back, *To infinity and beyond.*

"Iza! Can I go show Eek?" Max asks me referring to my brother.

I set him down and say, "Of course."

Max met Zeke during the playoffs and has taken to him ever since. It's both adorable and hilarious watching my big brother interact with Max.

Remy knocks on the glass, and I turn back to him. He's looking up at me with an expectant look on his face. I roll my eyes but pull out a small Ziploc bag of Hershey kisses for him.

Even though I've been back for a month or so, Remy told me it became part of his playoff routine. I understand his "superstitions" because I'm a hockey fan. I know what it's like having the thought that something helps you win.

Don't Atlanta it up, I mouth to him.

He just smiles and catches the bag before shaking his head and skating off.

Jake skates by and gives me pouty lips in turn I give him my middle finger. He smiles and goes back to warmups.

Three's only a minute left of the game and I'm biting my cheek. If the Flames can keep the Edmonton Panthers out of our goal zone, we'll be fine. We're up by one and I really don't want it to go to overtime. I know the guys don't have much steam left in them and there's no guarantee they'd be able to hold on.

We get the puck and Grant takes a shot. I hold my breath as I watch. The goal lights go off and we all scream in excitement.

The Flames just won the fucking Stanley Cup!

Remy skates by our section and I pretend to scream with excitement at him. A smile lights up his face, and he makes a subtle motion with his head, telling me to come down.

Our families and I hurry down to get on the ice.

Grant stops me before I can go find Remy and says, "He's in the locker room."

"Why?" I ask.

Grant shrugs and replies, "Don't know, but he said to tell you that's where he is."

"Okay."

Weird. I turn and make my way toward the locker room. As I open the door I play with my necklace.

I find Remy sitting in his cubby. I walk over to him as he looks up at me.

"What's wrong baby?" I ask stepping between his legs.

He takes my hand and replies, "Nothing's wrong. I just wanted to get you alone."

"Why?" I ask.

Remy grabs something behind him and stands as he says, "So I could do this."

He gets down on one knee and my mouth drops open.

"Eliza Grace Fox," Remy starts. "I know today is the thirteenth, but that's half of twenty-six, so I think it's still lucky."

He takes a deep breath before continuing, "I never really believed in love at first sight until I saw you for the first time. It didn't matter how fast things were moving with us because everything felt right.

"I want to spend an eternity with you Eliza Grace, infinity and beyond. Will you marry me?"

I throw my arms around his neck, almost causing him to fall as I exclaim, "Yes! A thousand fucking times, yes!"

I pull back and he places the ring on my left ring finger.

Pulling Remy up, I bring his mouth to mine. His hands find their way under my jersey, and he squeezes my hips.

Breaking the kiss Remy rests his forehead on mine as we both smile.

"We better get back out there," he says. "We have two things to celebrate now."

I don't think I stop smiling the rest of the night, but neither does Remy. And that's okay because like he said, we have two things to celebrate on this evening in Jus

Playlist

Dead Beat City - Kids That Fly

lipstick - jordan day, Promoting Sounds

(I Just) Died In Your Arms - Cutting Crew

Falling - Chase Atlantic

Best Friends - 5 Seconds of Summer

Rock Me - One Direction

Wildest Dream (Taylor's Version) - Taylor Swift

invisible string - Taylor Swift

Pretty Boy - The Neighbourhood

Electric Love - Børns

I Was Made For Lovin' You - YUNGBLUD

Lover Of Mine - 5 Seconds of Summer

Yours - Piper Hill

Love Story (Taylor's Version) - Taylor Swift

ACKNOWLEDGMENTS

First off let me start by saying, yes I know the Atlanta Flames were actually an NHL team in Atlanta. When I came up with the idea for this book it had not been my intention to name my team after the Flames, but once I realized that I named this team after the original Atlanta Flames, I decided to just roll with it and give the team some redemption as well as a new life.

This story came to me randomly and sat in the notes app on my phone as "Film Editor x Hockey Player" for a good minute. But the more I thought about it the more I kept adding to the note, and finally I sat down with a notebook and pen to being writing. There were many times that I didn't think that this story would actually turn into anything. Honestly multiple times I thought that I would lose interest in it, but the more I kept going the more I fell in love with it.

To my fellow Atlanta sports fans, I know it's hard to be a fan sometimes because our sports teams are more times than not a disappointment. Trust me I know how it feels for our Atlanta Braves to take thirty years in between World Series wins. I also know what it's like rooting for the Atlanta Gladiators only for them to never meet expectations. I even know what it feels like rooting for the Atlanta Falcons when they went to the Super Bowl in 2017, only for them to fumble it. The good news though, is that this book is a work of fiction and that means I can make an Atlanta sports team win. So thank you for bearing with me as we went on this journey together, because at the end of the day this hockey team was able to win the Stanley Cup.

To my friends and family, I'm sorry for keeping this from you. I know I would've had your unwavering support, but I think this was something that I needed to do for myself before telling anyone. That being said if you actually read *Lights, Camera, Crosscheck* please don't talk to me about it, because I don't need to know that you know about the kind of stuff I write. Even if this is decently tame, please don't mention it to me.

To my friend Piper, thank you for writing some songs that are really amazing. Just know that I wanted to put "Window" on the playlist for this one, but it didn't fit the vibe. But don't worry I have plans for it. With that being said, I'm so glad that you wrote "Yours," and that Micah is good enough for you to be able to write a happy love song.

To my readers, thank you so much for indulging in this little editor's idea. Without you I don't think there would be Eliza and Remy in the way they are now. Knowing someone might read this book really helped me to get the ideas out of my head and onto a word document, so for that I thank you.

ABOUT THE AUTHOR

As a Georgia native, L. Wood is used to being disappointed by Georgia sports teams, but that doesn't stop her from enjoying them. While she doesn't know all of the rules of hockey, she loves attending games and watching either the Atlanta Gladiators or the Athens Rock Lobsters as they take on their opponents in their respective leagues. She graduated from the University of North Georgia with a BFA in Film & Digital Media, but has always had a passion for writing and telling stories. By day L. Wood is an aspiring editor trying to break into the film industry, by night she spends her time writing fictional love stories that she hopes to share with the world. L. Wood creates stories that sometimes stem from her own personal experiences, but allow for everyone to relate to them in some way while making it enjoyable.

instagram.com/authorl.wood